Target Nina
Ground Zero

A Few Good Men
Book Two

Jessika Klide Writing as Stingray23

Author's Copyright

This is a work of fiction. Names, characters, organizations, places, events, and incidents are either products of the author's imagination or are used fictitiously. Any resemblance to actual events, locales, or persons living or dead are entirely coincidental.

Copyright © 2022 Stingray23 ALL RIGHTS RESERVED

No part of this book may be reproduced, or stored in a retrieval system, or transmitted in any form or by any means electronic, mechanical, photocopying, recording, or otherwise, without express written permission of the publisher.

This book is licensed for your personal enjoyment only. This book may not be re-sold or given away to other people.

Editing by: Maria Clark

Published in the United States of America

HUMAN TRAFFICKING HAPPENS EVERYWHERE. TO MEN, WOMEN, AND CHILDREN OF ALL AGES, RACES, NATIONALITIES, AND GENDERS.

DONATE TO MAKE A DIFFERENCE: OURRESCUE.ORG

IF YOU OR SOMEONE YOU KNOW IS A VICTIM OF HUMAN TRAFFICKING, REACH OUT FOR HELP OR REPORT A TIP NOW.

NATIONAL HUMAN TRAFFICKING HOTLINE
1-888-373-7888

TEXT **"BEFREE"** OR **"HELP"** TO **233733**

EMAIL: HELP@HUMANTRAFFICKINGHOTLINE.ORG

NATIONAL CENTER FOR MISSING OR EXPLOITED CHILDREN
1-800-THE-LOST

Contents

The Navy Seal Creed	7
Chapter 1	15
Chapter 2	27
Chapter 3	37
Chapter 4	45
Chapter 5	51
Chapter 6	57
Chapter 7	65
Chapter 8	77
Chapter 9	87
Chapter 10	93
Chapter 11	101
Chapter 12	113
Chapter 13	123
Chapter 14	135
Chapter 15	145
Chapter 16	153
Chapter 17	161
Chapter 18	169
Chapter 19	177
Epilogue	187

Jessika writing as Stingray23	203
Jessika writing as Cindee Bartholomew	205
Read Jessika's newest, sexiest, and most talked about bestsellers...	207
Stingray23	211
Stingray23.com	213

The Navy Seal Creed

In times of war or uncertainty there is a special breed of warrior ready to answer our Nation's call. A common man with uncommon desire to succeed.

Forged by adversity, he stands alongside America's finest special operations forces to serve his country, the American people, and protect their way of life.

I am that man.

My Trident is a symbol of honor and heritage. Bestowed upon me by the heroes that have gone before, it embodies the trust of those I have sworn to protect. By wearing the Trident, I accept the responsibility of my chosen profession and way of life. It is a privilege that I must earn every day.

My loyalty to Country and Team is beyond reproach. I humbly serve as a guardian to my fellow Americans always ready to defend those who are unable to defend themselves. I do not advertise the nature of my work, nor seek recognition for my actions. I voluntarily accept the inherent hazards of my profession, placing the welfare and security of others before my own.

I serve with honor on and off the battlefield. The ability to control my emotions and my actions, regardless of circumstance, sets me apart from other men.

Uncompromising integrity is my standard. My character and honor are steadfast. My word is my bond.

We expect to lead and be led. In the absence of orders, I will take charge, lead my teammates, and accomplish the mission. I lead by example in all situations.

I will never quit. I persevere and

thrive on adversity. My Nation expects me to be physically harder and mentally stronger than my enemies. If knocked down, I will get back up, every time. I will draw on every remaining ounce of strength to protect my teammates and to accomplish our mission. I am never out of the fight.

We demand discipline. We expect innovation. The lives of my teammates and the success of our mission depend on me — my technical skill, tactical proficiency, and attention to detail. My training is never complete.

We train for war and fight to win. I stand ready to bring the full spectrum of combat power to bear in order to achieve my mission and the goals established by my country. The execution of my duties will be swift and violent when required yet guided by the very principles that I serve to defend.

Brave men have fought and died building the proud tradition and feared reputation that I am bound to uphold.

In the worst of conditions, the legacy of my teammates steadies my resolve and silently guides my every deed.

I will not fail.

Everything happens for a reason is complete bullshit.

Everything happens because of individual choices in the collective whole and the decisions made.

Make good choices.
Make better decisions.

— — Jeff 'Rocket' Crockett

Target Nina

One
Part One

San Diego, California
March 2010
7:00 *AM*

———

Crockett

———

"Rocket, there's an issue with the beer delivery."

That's the way my morning started at 4:00 o'clock. Instead of heading out for my daily five-mile run, I was in the bar stock room unloading a brand of beer I didn't order but had to accept because my stock was too low to return it.

Three and a half hours later, my schedule is back on track to pound the pavement. It's 7:35 am. I hit the stopwatch on my g-shock watch to track my time as I hit my cruising gait, exiting the parking lot of *Suds After BUD/S* Bar.

The highway traffic isn't congested yet. However, it is heavy enough and will only intensify as rush-hour approaches. It'll be safer running through the residential area this time of day. Parents are more aware of pedestrians with school buses and carpools.

Good choice, I phrase myself as I cruise between the streets and the sidewalks, leaving the first subdivision behind and entering the second one.

As soon as I run through the entrance, I spot a white work van, and my SEAL sixth sense alarm bells go off. It's out of place. Granted, it may be a work crew arriving early to repair someone's plumbing or an electrical issue, but my gut tells me it isn't.

I jog onto the sidewalk and stop behind a tree to observe without being seen.

There are no identifying markings on the side of the van. Two men have their forearms resting in the open windows. Nothing unusual or alarming. Except they are wearing black hoodies, and it's not cool this morning.

Not convinced I'm wrong yet, I hang back to observe them.

In the next few minutes, the neighborhood comes alive with organized chaos as adults and children exit their homes. Some load into their vehicles and drive away. While others hang out in their front yards, waiting for their ride to pick them up, chatting with their next-door neighbors, or looking at their phones. All are unaware that danger may be lurking in the white van. No one pays it any attention.

When the school bus turns onto the street at the opposite end of the block, children move to the curb along the street, waiting for their turn to board the bus.

As soon as the van's engine comes to life and the brake lights glow an ominous warning, years of extensive training as a SEAL kick in, and the hair on the back of my neck rises as I identify the intentions of the men in the van. This is a brazen snatch-and-grab in broad daylight.

I scan the neighborhood for their target. Two houses away, I spot her. A young pre-teen girl slings a heavy backpack onto her shoulders and moves to her designated pickup point.

There is time to let my presence be known and scare the would-be kidnappers away before they make their move, and as a civilian, I should make that choice. But I also know that doing so will, more than likely, *not* be a deterrent from a future attempt. It's quite possible they will just move to a different neighborhood when I've moved on.

Or do I sit tight and let them hang the crime around their necks? Then stop them before they can get away? It's tough because this choice leads to the young girl being traumatized but safe.

I pull my weapon from my shoulder holster and wait behind the tree, watching how they will carry out their mission.

I have no official authority to act in any capacity. But I can't turn off who I am. I'm a special warfare operator trained to defend Americans' right to live free and to protect those who cannot protect themselves. I will continue to serve as a guardian of freedom.

The bright red brake lights vanish as the van

begins to creep forward. The young girl is looking at her phone, oblivious to her surroundings, as she stops at the edge of the curb.

That's when all hell breaks loose. The side sliding door and the passenger cab door swing open, and two men bail out, charging the unsuspecting girl.

The calm of battle settles over me as my training controls my response to their chaos. Every sense is heightened. Every movement is composed—every decision is backed by discipline.

When the men are a few feet away from her, she looks up from her phone. Shocked, she freezes. Before she can flee, they are on her.

The first man dry-tases her, and she jerks from the jolt of electricity, dropping her phone. Momentarily stunned, the shift of her backpack's weight causes her young, underdeveloped body rigged from the voltage to keel over.

My subconscious begins a count of her trauma to exact vengeance for her. They will pay for that.

The men each grab an arm and drag her toward the van. She regains her wits and starts kicking and screaming, putting up one hell of a fight for a little thing, and the commotion she's causing is the perfect cover for me to rush up to the back of the van unseen.

The entire crew is focused on getting the flailing girl fighting for her life inside the vehicle as fast as possible so they can disappear with her when I step around the side of the van. In two strides, I'm next to her, with my weapon pointed less than three feet from the face of the man inside who is hoisting her in by her hair.

"Hooyah, Motherfuckers, not on my watch."

The driver of the van yells, "WHAT THE FUCK?"

As the three men attacking her freeze with surprise, then fear. Their grips loosen. The frightened, fighting girl breaks free, fleeing to the safety of her home, screaming for her mama.

The driver of the van yells again, "SHIT!"

Staring at my pistol pointed at his frozen accomplices, his eyes flare in fear, then flash panic right before he makes a deadly decision, reaching for his pistol lying on the center console. As his hand encircles it, I hit him with a single shot between his eyes. His head snaps back as the bullet enters, then recoils forward from the force of his skull exploding. His brain splatters on the steering wheel and windshield.

Nina

Standing at the front door, watching Jeff Crockett hold three men at gunpoint outside a white van parked at the curb while Bethany, my twelve-year-old niece, races across the yard to us, calling her mama like a three-year-old, is the biggest mind fuck of my life.

We were sitting at the kitchen table, enjoying a cup of coffee, discussing our plans for the day, when we heard a gunshot. The sound sent a wave of sheer terror through us, and we jumped to our feet, then charged the front door. Our lives forever changed.

In shock on multiple levels, I'm rooted to the spot. Maternal emotion for the girl I love, as if she were my own, dumps adrenaline in my blood while fierce passion for the man I love who is in danger courses through my veins. Ultimately, my training kicks in to assess the situation.

Bethany is safe in Bri's arms. Crockett has the perps apprehended. I step back inside and usher my sister and niece in, closing the door on the team leader of Alpha. The man that I served alongside as their targeting officer. The man I fell in love with, but the man who never knew due to military restrictions against relationships between team members.

Now is not the time for a reunion with Crockett. Now my family comes first.

Crockett

Immediately, my weapon returns to my first target's face, and sheer terror stares back at me. A dark wet spot grows at his groin. He's pissed himself.

Before any of the remaining three choose to make a deadly decision, I command them, "Put your hands on your head. Interlace your fingers."

In shock and fear, they do what they are told.

"Step out of the van. Drop to your knees."

They obey, but I know the adrenaline rush will hit them at any moment, and nature will make them choose fight or flight, and I prepare to pull the trigger again.

Taking a commanding, menacing step toward them to counteract their adrenaline dump, I give them their only option. "Kiss the ground that little girl walked on, and don't fucking move a goddamn muscle, or I will blow your fucking brains out like your compadre's there. Do you understand?"

The forcefulness of my vow makes them fall on their faces, and we wait for the police to arrive without further incident.

Nina

While Bri comforts her daughter, I watch from the window as the men lie face down with Rocket standing guide over them, waiting for the police to arrive. He's a beautiful sight to behold. Standing there in all his SEAL glory with the situation under control.

My heart flutters watching him, confirming my fear that even after years apart, he's the one that rocks my world. I look at my niece, safe in my sister's arms, and dread the inevitable outcome. I must thank Rocket for rescuing my niece. But I honestly don't know if my broken heart can take the face-off with him if it leads to nothing more than friendship. I am and always will be in love with him.

Crockett

In no time, two police cruisers are on site.

As soon as the police officers exit their vehicles, I drop to my knees, place my weapon on the ground, and put my hands on my head, interlocking my fingers.

After the police take control of the chaos, I

give my statement, and witnesses come forward, reiterating what I have testified.

Before I leave, I look at the little girl's house. She and her mother stand in the doorway, watching, and someone else is standing in the shadow at the window. The young girl raises her hand to wave a silent thank you, and I raise mine in response.

Freedom is always worth fighting for.

Two

Crockett

―――

SITTING AT MY TABLE IN *SUDS AFTER BUD/S* de-stressing over a glass of whiskey, the lead detective calls to inform me that I will not be charged for killing the pervert. The men I apprehended confirmed my testimony and confessed that they were not targeting the girl specifically, just targeting young girls. Their intention was to smuggle her over the border into Mexico, then sell her into sex trafficking.

I thank him for the call, slam down the remaining whiskey in my glass and think about the numbers he threw out. They were staggering. "Estimates of 40 million people are enslaved across the world every year, and 79% of those involve sexual exploitation. Due to the fact that individuals are transported across borders, it makes it especially difficult for law enforcement to investigate and rescue them. The average age is twenty-seven years old."

I pour myself another shot of booze, swirl the amber liquid in the glass, and mull over the idea that formed while he was talking.

Freedom is never free. It requires constant vigilance and a willingness to take up arms to defend it. I may not be fighting any longer for the cause as part of the military under the direction of the President, but that doesn't mean I can't fight for it on a civilian level.

I sip the dark water and stretch my legs under the table as the idea of starting a private security company specializing in rescuing victims of trafficking solidifies.

There are plenty of companies that hire former special warfare operators as bodyguards. But I am not aware of a single one that offers its services to combat human trafficking directly. We have the skills to search and rescue victims taken, and saving the girl today wasn't my first time.

I will never forget the desperation in Butch Wofford's voice when he called and told me his son and his girlfriend had been taken hostage in Africa while on a mission trip. The kidnappers demanded more money than Butch was willing to gamble on his son's life.

"Crockett, I'm calling in the debt you said you owed me."

Within twenty-four hours, I had an extraction team of former SEALs on a jet flying across the ocean. We went in, did a snatch-and-grab, and safely brought the couple home.

Why would I not offer other families that service?

I pull my phone out of my pocket to type in my notes a list of Pros versus Cons. The first pro is fresh on my mind. "Saving innocent girls from becoming sex slaves."

The name Coq Blockers pops into my brain, and I smirk; the guys will love it. Nothing like a group of badass motherfuckers to block the cocks of sexual deviants and perverted sickos.

The next pro is "Getting the team back together."

The first person that always comes to mind when I remember my time as Alpha 1 isn't my brothers. It's Nina Fox. Our targeting officer. The woman I've always wanted but could never have. Mission restrictions forbade it.

I swirl the amber liquid and ponder everything forming my own company could mean. It would mean Nina would not be off-limits. I drain the glass, then pour another shot.

Foxtrot. I fell in love with her the first time I laid eyes on her. It was just before nine pm on a Tuesday night in a bar in Virginia Beach about six years ago. Mike Franks, my number two, Jocko, my number four at the time, and I were wrapping up a steak dinner when three beautiful women walked in.

Nina caught my eye immediately. She was gorgeous with big eyes, a great smile, and an easy laugh. Her thick black hair was one length, cropped along her neckline, longer in the front than the back, and angled to frame her beautiful face. Her blouse hugged her full, not fake, tits. The neckline was extra wide and exposed her flawless skin. Her bra offered them up invitingly. The rounded tops and deep cleavage pushed my buttons.

They sat across the room at a table, and my position gave me a great view. I locked in on the target.

The waiter took their order, and when he walked away, she scanned the room. Our eyes met, and boom, sparks. The connection was instant and electric.

I ask my brothers, "Either of you feel like getting fucked tonight?"

Jocko cut his eyes at me, confused. His back was to them so they weren't on his radar yet. "Fucked or fucked up?" He clarified.

I nodded in the direction of the girls.

He and Mike, not so subtly, turned and looked at the same time. Nina smirked at us, then leaned over to say something to her girlfriends.

I piped up first, "Dibs on the raven-haired beauty."

Mike's choice was "Dibs on the redhead."

Jocko chuckled, "Blonde's have more fun, boys." Then he said, "Luce, go introduce yourself."

His black Belgian Malinois got up from under the table and trotted over. Of course, the women fawned over him with 'ooh's and ah's,' and we followed behind, pulling over additional chairs to sit with them.

After about an hour of laughing our asses off at Mike's impromptu entertainment, Nina announced she had a big day tomorrow and needed to get home.

She stood, and I stood too, offering to walk her out, but she shot me down. "Sorry. SEALs are off limits."

"Who said I was a SEAL?" I teased her.

Her eyebrow cocked, and an expression I later termed her 'NBA' for 'no-bullshit-allowed' barred any hope of lying my way through her filter and into her bed.

The next morning, I learned why SEALs were off-limits. She walked into the war room in fatigues and boots. She was our new targeting officer, and I was fucked, but not like I wanted. Being romantically involved with a team member was strictly forbidden.

As a Tier One Operator, there are inherent professional hazards, and Nina Fox became one of mine that day. In all the years she and I worked together, I never let on how I felt about her. She never knew how much I wanted to spend every free moment making love to her.

Hiding those feelings for her tested my integrity and discipline to the max. It was hard as hell and never got any easier. The spark between us never went away.

She did, however, know how much I respected her. She was damn good at her job, and I made sure she knew I knew.

When I left the military, I thought long and hard about hitting on her and hooking up. But she was still serving with Alpha, and I couldn't take the chance that she would be distracted from the mission for any reason.

I toss back my shot and pour another. She still haunts my fucking dreams.

I swirl the liquid and smile. This time I will be the one who sets the code of conduct, and in the civilian world, there are no restrictions. No reason not to be together.

So, the first name I type in my list is Nina Fox. Then, I list the special warfare operators and other support personnel I intend to recruit.

When the list is complete, I toast my decision. "HOOYAH!"

Nina

Snuggled up on the couch together, Bri, Bethany, and I binge on Netflix movies, staying focused on comedies and nothing serious or dramatic, munching on chips and popcorn.

When Bethany finally drifts off to sleep, Bri whispers, "Nina, do you think she was targeted specifically?"

I shake my head. "No, I don't think so."

"Good." She says as she strokes her baby's hair. Then after a moment, she asks, "Why?"

I look at her stressed face. "Why do I think she wasn't targeted specifically?"

She nods.

"Because if they wanted Bethany, there are other places to snatch her that would have been easier to get away. They were cruising the streets, looking for a random target. If not her, then someone else would have been grabbed."

Her face is frozen with fear. "What other places?" She asks.

I smile. "Don't go there in this state. You're emotionally traumatized right now. We'll discuss the entire situation later in detail when you are both clear-headed. I'll teach you both some defensive hand-to-hand combat tactics too."

She nods, then adds, "I'm so thankful you were here. I wouldn't have handled this very well alone."

"I am too." I lean over and squeeze her hand.

She says, "And that dude that saved her! What would have happened if he hadn't stepped in?"

I laugh, "I would have unloaded a full magazine clip on them."

She laughs, "You're such a badass, sis."

I shrug, "It's true. I would have gone ballistic, but when I saw Crockett had it under control, I knew I wasn't needed."

"Crockett? You know him?"

I nod my head. "Yes, we served together in the military. I was the targeting officer for Alpha, and he was the team leader."

"My god! And I worried about you all those years. If I had only known...." She laughs. "What are the odds he would be the one who was in the right place at the right time?"

"Astronomical, for sure."

"We have to thank him for what he did."

"I know, but...." I grab the remote to pick

another movie.

"But..." she waits for my answer.

"But later. Not right away."

"Why not?" She asks suspiciously.

"Truthfully, sister. I need time to wrap my head around seeing him again in civilian life without the barrier of military restrictions between us."

"Mmmhmm," she eyes me. "You two wanted too but couldn't?"

"It's one-sided," I smirk at her. "My side."

She says, "You're hesitant? Why?"

"I don't know if my heart can handle a flat-out rejection. It's been cracked for so long."

"Well," she says, "thanking him isn't exactly you throwing yourself at his feet. It's just opening a closed door of opportunity."

I sigh, "I know, but if he only treats me as a former teammate, it'll be just as broken."

"So, it's love, not attraction."

I nod. "Afraid so."

"Ok." She says, "I understand."

"How about this classic?" I ask her.

"Sure," she agrees.

And we settle in to watch the 1990 version of Teenage Mutant Ninja Turtles. "Cowabunga!"

Three

Crockett

———

Meghan Meadows is behind the counter and speaks, "Good morning, Rocket. Have a good run."

I throw my hand up, acknowledging her comment. "Morning, Ambassador." I jog in place at the entrance while the sliding doors open, then I hit the pavement as the first rays of the sun break the horizon.

Rather than returning to my regular early morning routine, I decided to run yesterday's route, wanting to revisit the street where all the shit went down. My breath syncs to the pounding of my feet on the pavement as my mind mulls the details of making Coq Blockers a reality.

By the time I turn onto the street, the sun is up, but the neighborhood is still asleep. When I am ten houses away from the home where the young girl lives, the front door opens, and a female steps outside dressed in a compression shirt that firmly hugs her nice size tits and tight running pants with reflective stripes down the sides that accentuates the sweet curvature of a nice ass.

She takes a deep breath, lifts her hands over her head, clasps them together, and stretches. My feet stumble, and I come to a jarring stop.

What in the fuck? It can't be! ...Foxtrot?

She lowers her hands, sets them on her hips, and rotates her head on her shoulders like I've seen her do thousands of times to reduce stress.

What are the fucking odds that the woman I love would come out of the house of the little girl I rescued? I run my fingers through my hair. Beyond fucking astronomical!

She takes off for her morning run, trotting down the short drive. My mind kicks into overdrive, working the problem for the best possible outcome. If she turns left and comes toward me, I'll simply stand here and wait for her to recognize me. But if she turns right, I'll have to chase her down.

She turns right, and I take off after her. She's running at a good clip, so catching up takes some time, and I keep grinning at this stroke of good fortune.

Adjusting my longer stride to sync with hers, I admire her long legs and firm ass. She is heavier than the last time I saw her. Which I love. More curves.

Her thick silky black hair is in a ponytail and swings like a pendulum with the rhythm of her pace. It's the kind of hair that kicks you in your gut with a sweet sensation when you wrap your hand in it to take control. Damn straight. That!

I fall in behind her, keeping a safe distance, waiting for the right moment to overtake her, and a cadence sounds off.

I don't know, but I've been told ....
Nina Fox is solid gold ....
Be it wrong or be it right ....
Nina Fox gets fucked tonight ....

I laugh. Finally! It's going to happen with

her, and the depth of the feeling is going to hit me right where it counts. No more empty fucks for the sake of physical necessity. From now on, fucking Foxtrot will be exclusive.

As we approach the corner of the block, I prepare to overtake her based on the choice of her route. If she doesn't stop, I'll overtake her. If she stops, I'll jog up next to her. God, I can't wait to see her reaction.

She slows when she reaches the corner, so I'm only twenty feet behind her, ready to confront her. But then she takes a sharp, hard ninety-degree right turn and sprints, putting distance between us.

I chuckle. *Of course, she felt me behind her, targeting her.*

She turns her head to catch a glimpse of who's trailer her, and I smile. Busted.

Nina

SHIT! It's Rocket! SHIT! SHIT! SHIT!

I panic, but I slow down, knowing the reunion is out of my control. It will be here.... Sweaty. *Fuck my luck!*

I come to a stop, put my hands on my hips, and wait to be treated as an old platonic friend. My heart begins to rip in two.

When he pulls alongside me, I stare at the ground, bracing myself. He moves close, invading my space. The tips of his sneakers come into view.

I slowly lift my eyes to his, taking in every breathtaking beautiful muscle of his physical perfection. His long straight legs, his 'package' that's secured in compression shorts, his small trim waistline, his hard abs, the sharp angle up to his broad shoulders, his plump pecs.

He's wearing that cute 'devil be damned' grin that makes a dimple in his cheek, and my heart turns to total mush. The twinkle in his eyes sends butterflies soaring around my gut like I'm a teenager. The spark that has always been there doesn't flare. It erupts into a raging fire of exigency.

My God, he is a handsome son of a bitch!

His boyish shit-eating grin rocks my world. I smile back, unable to deny him the joy my heart holds to be with him again. But his eyes belie the lightness of his thoughts.

They hone in on mine with the insane intensity he wore when he focused on the mission, zoning in on his target, and every cell in my body tunes in, desperate to be consumed by him. Right here. Right now! We've wasted enough time with dutiful deferential behavior.

Crockett

Staring into Nina's eyes without the need to hold back how I feel about her has got to the most liberating experience of my life. Bar none, and that's quite a statement coming from the top man of elite special warfare operators.

She is more beautiful than I remember. Her coffee-colored eyes bore into my soul, searching for a clue as to how to handle this impromptu reunion.

The air between us feels alive, and the grin that I've been wearing since I spotted her deepens as my cock gets hard at the thought that nothing stands between us now. I can pull her into my arms, slide my hands inside her shirt to feel her soft silky skin while I bury my nose in her neck, and whisper how happy I am to see her again.

Yet, her expression is unnerving. This woman staring up at me isn't the tough-as-nails disciplined targeting officer that kept me at arm's length for both our own good. This woman is vulnerable, and her expression makes my balls draw up tight to hold the semen building as my cock gets rock hard. The knowledge that I am free to let my desire overwhelm me and that she won't resist is a force of nature I'm unprepared to handle. Her submissive demeanor is heady and stokes the embers of love that have been burning for her since the first time I laid eyes on her.

I smile as the mental leash I've controlled my inner beast with falls away. There is no need to stop the storm brewing inside now. I can relax and let my feelings for her show. She needs to know how much she means to me, but words are weak and won't work.

Four

"Hey." The softness in my voice surprises me.

Her response is a breathless, "Rocket."

"Foxtrot, you look good."

Man, does she ever!

My gut tightens with the emotion, and I take a step closer. Her eyes dart back and forth from one to the other of mine, searching my soul, waiting for me to take the lead.

I don't ask how she is doing. I can see she is doing just fine.

I don't ask what she has been up to. It doesn't matter. She is here now.

I ask what is essential to know before

choosing which path to go down. Friendship or lovers.

"Are you involved with anyone?"

She blinks, surprised, I suppose, at the directness of my question and asks, "Why?"

"Two reasons," I smirk.

She smirks back, knowing me well enough to know I am setting her up for something. "What are they?"

I take another step forward, and her head tilts, wary of my advance, but she stands her ground. My smirk deepens.

"One, I have a job offer for you."

The shock on her face is real, and it throws her off her game, which is why I went with it first. I take another step closer.

"After what happened yesterday, I've decided to start a private security company to fight human trafficking, and I'm going to hire as many former members of Alpha as I can. And, babe, you are at the top of the list."

Her jaw falls open. "What?"

"And two, I'm not."

She shakes her head to clear the overload, then she frowns, and I nearly laugh. Of all the things she and I have been through together, that frown is the most severe I've ever seen her pretty face wear, which makes the smirk on my face seriously hurt.

"You're not what?"

I look her up and down and say, "I'm not involved with anyone at the moment, so, if you're not, then there is no reason for me to stifle my feelings for you any longer."

The shock on her face returns, and I cannot help the chuckle that teases her. I am on fucking cloud nine right now. "Well, Foxtrot? Are you available for me to hit on, or are you still off-limits?"

As the implications of what I am saying to her dawn on her, the change in her expression is phenomenal and takes my breath away. Not only is she willing, but she is relieved.

I step forward, reaching for her face and tilt it up to mine. I stare into her eyes and caress her soul, for what I hope she feels is forever because that is what I am aiming for.

Then I slowly lower my mouth to hers, and when I taste her sweetness for the very first time, I know I will never taste another woman again. I will do whatever it takes to make Nina Fox mine.

Her lips are soft and sensuously part to let

my tongue slip inside her to claim her. The ache in my heart is real, and this time, it is from the fullness it feels knowing she is my final conquest.

Her hands tentatively touch my chest as if she longs to caress it but is scared it isn't real. Her timidness drives me crazy with both want and need to dominate her, to let her know that I am a starving man, and to assure her that only she can satisfy me.

I make my intentions clear. Sliding one hand down her back and grabbing her ass, while the other one wraps itself in her ponytail, jerking her head back, as I pull her body against my erection.

The more power I assert over her, the more she relaxes in my arms, and when I thrust my tongue deep into her mouth, she opens wide and sucks it down her throat.

The primal growl that I hear myself make in response as her hands slip around my waist, down over my ass, and flex on my buttocks is sheer carnal caveman.

A truck horn toots three short pops, then sits on it, blasting the air as it passes us. I force myself to gain control over my feelings, but it is damn hard to do.

My hands move to the top of her shoulders and grip them, then I release her lips. She looks wild and free with her flushed cheeks. Her pent-up passion matching my own.

"I have wanted to do that since the first time I saw you."

She stares up at me, panting. Her chest heaving. Her taut nipples pressing against her compression shirt, wanting to be released, wanting to be fondled and adored.

My cock is so fucking hard it hurts, and I look around for a place for us to fuck. Across the street is a five-foot chain-link fence surrounding a baseball field. That will do.

Five

Crockett

———

"Hey." The softness in my voice surprises me.

Her response is breathless, "Rocket."

"Foxtrot, you look good."

Man, does she ever!

My gut tightens with the emotion, and I take a step closer. Her eyes dart back and forth from one to the other of mine, searching my soul, waiting for me to take the lead.

I don't ask how she is doing. I can see she is doing just fine.

I don't ask what she has been up to. It doesn't matter. She is here now.

I ask what is essential to know before choosing which path to go down. Friendship or lovers? I have to hear her say it. She has to give me permission. There must be no misunderstanding or miscommunication between us. We have to be united on this.

"Are you involved with anyone?" My breath pauses, waiting for her answer.

She blinks. She's surprised by the question. I suppose, at the directness of it and the desperation hidden in it. She blurts back, "Why?"

"Two reasons," I smirk, taking another small step toward her, wanting my intention known.

She smirks back, knowing me well enough to know I am setting her up for something. "What are your two reasons?"

I take another small step forward, leaving only a couple of inches between us. She stands her ground, tilting her face up to mine, staring unblinkingly into my eyes. The strong, independent woman I know prepares for the battle ahead.

My smirk deepens. "One, I have a job offer for you."

The shock on her face is real, and it throws her off her passive-aggressive game. I lean to tower over her, and the breath she takes is filled with my pheromones.

I explain further, "After what happened yesterday, I'm starting a private security company to fight human trafficking, and I'm going to hire as many former members of Alpha as I can."

She blinks as she absorbs the business offer, but I see fear settle in her eyes. "Oh," she whispers, taking a step back to put distance between us. Her reaction breaks my heart.

"Two...." I stalk her again, closing the distance to inches, towering over her, needing her to know I'm only holding back because I need her to choose.

"If you're not involved with anyone, there is no reason for me to stifle my feelings for you any longer."

Boom! That hit her heart.

"If you're not involved with anyone, I'm free to make a play for you."

I touch her face and trace my fingertip down her cheek. "I want to show you what you mean to me."

She stares into my eyes, caressing my soul with them.

The moment is finally here. It's time to taste her, to brand her, to claim her. I slowly lower my mouth to hers, and when her sweetness mingles, then merges with me for the very first time, I know I have found my forever.

Her lips are soft and sensually part, inviting me in. My tongue slips gently past her barriers to claim her. The ache in my heart is real, but this time, it is from the fullness of knowing she is mine.

Her hands timidly touch my waist, and the need to crush my cock inside her hurts. My tongue becomes more demanding. Sliding one hand down her back and grabbing her ass, the other one wraps itself in her lush ponytail. Jerking her head back, I yank her body against my full, hard, throbbing erection.

Her response speaks volumes. The more power I assert over her, the more she relaxes in my arms, knowing she belongs here. When I thrust my tongue deep into her mouth, she clamps her mouth around it and sucks it down her throat.

The primal growl I hear myself make as her

hands grip my waist, then knead their way around my waist, down over my cheeks to flex and constrict my ass is sheer carnal caveman.

A truck horn toots three short pops, then honks continuously, blasting the air as it passes us. Her mouth breaks free, and I'm forced to gain control over myself. But it is damn hard to do!

My hands grip the top of her shoulders as I focus on her face. Her cheeks are flushed. Her eyes are wild. She looks fucking free!

My eyes take in everything. She's panting. Her chest is heaving. Her taut nipples press against her compression shirt, wanting to be released, wanting to be fondled and adored.

My cock is so fucking hard it hurts, and I look around for a private place for us to fuck.

The floodgates are open. All the years of frustration washed away in an instant. Our love won't be denied another minute. Consummation is at hand.

Across the street is a five-foot chain-link fence surrounding a baseball field. That will do.

I grab her and frogmarch her across the street. She goes willingly, but I wasn't asking. I'm taking what's mine. Claiming her. Erasing everyone else. Leaving no doubt or room for fear inside her ever again. She will KNOW because I have SHOWED her.

At the fence, I scoop her up into my arms and set her on the other side, then I put both hands on the top bar of the fence and spring over.

As soon as my feet land, she slips her hand in mine. The compliance she freely gives....

We make our way to the grandstand area. I don't want to take her in a rush under the bleachers if I don't have to. I try a door, and it opens. I step in, and she follows close behind. I shut the door and turn the lock. The world outside vanishes.

Six

Crockett

———

When I turn around, her top is coming off. Her arms are crossed over her head, bound by the fabric covering her face.

My heart soars with her lack of inhibition. This confident, strong, independent woman that I love, loves me. She's as ready to prove it as I am.

Her gorgeous tits are bare and vulnerable, begging me to devour them. I hear my growl again as I close the distance to her. Then with one arm around her, I jerk her body roughly to mine and cup a breast with my hand, kneading the soft flesh. Her fight with the fabric pauses, as I lower my lips to suckle the elongated tip begging for my attention.

She gasps with pleasure, arching her back, offering them to my tongue. Her sexy as fuck moan echoes against the harsh concrete walls, and pre-cum seeps out of the tip of my cock.

When I move to the other breast, she untangles herself from the shirt and drops it on the ground. I squeeze her ass as I tease both nipples. One with my mouth and one pinched between my fingers. Her head falls back, and her knees buckle.

My hand grips a handful of her ass as my arm tightens around her waist, and I secure her limp body. My mouth moves from one tit to the other until she claws my back and lifts her head to watch.

Her husky, breathy voice begs me. "Rocket, please!"

I lift her off her feet, and as I carry her to the counter, I thrust my tongue back down her throat. She moans, and it is a sexy-as-fuck sound I'm already addicted to.

When I set her on top of the cold surface, she leans back and kicks her shoes off. I bend over to remove my weapon from my ankle harness and lay it on the counter next to her. Then my shirt comes off and covers it.

Her eyes flare at the sight of my muscles, and she whispers, "My God, you are gorgeous."

"I have waited for years for this moment, and I can't wait any longer." I reach for the waist of her pants, and she lifts her butt off the surface. With one hard tug, I strip her ass naked.

Her beauty is breathtaking. Her dark hair, neatly trimmed, matches her eyebrows. As she shifts her position so she hangs over the edge, my cock thumps of its own accord. I step up, unable to wait, and enter her zone as she spreads her legs wide.

I shove my pants down, and the infamous 'rocket' springs out. Her eyes flare again. "My. God," falls out of her mouth in a sexy gasp.

I lean over and capture her mouth with mine, pulling her further off the edge. Her long legs wrap around me, ready, and her hands caress my arms and shoulders. As her heels dig into my ass, pulling me in. I grab my cock, "Ready, baby?"

"Ohh, yes!" She says as she leans away. I slide it once down her slit to wet it, and she moans.

Then I line it up to hammer it home, placing the tip on the rim.

As I slowly insert myself inside her, her expression matches mine. Eager, hungry, anticipation.

As her velvety softness engulfs my rigid hardness, at the same moment, we express the ecstasy we share. "Ahhh."

My legs tremble with the sensation, and hers quiver, with every inch easing into her, becoming one. "Oh, baby, you feel so fucking good," I whisper, cradling her body to mine.

She buries her face in my neck, opens her mouth, and sucks the sensitive skin. Then she's devouring me with both her mouth and her pussy, kissing as she fucks.

Up and down my shaft, she works. I cup her ass with my hands and lean back, holding my hips in a flex, giving her full access to every inch of dick I have. She rides my cock with the rhythm she needs, and when she's ready to come, whimpering with need, I help her stroke herself to an explosion. Her legs tremor uncontrollably with her orgasm as she loses who she is to me.

When she collapses, I hold myself deep inside her and place little butterfly kisses on her shoulders while she recuperates. Ready to go again, she positions herself, resting her forehead on mine. "Go, baby," she says, "Your turn."

I peck her lips, lifting her back onto the counter, then climb up on top of her. I go down on her, gliding in and out. The velvety softness feels so incredible, and her sweet breath mixing with mine as she kisses my face drives me.

Careful not to be too rough with her, it doesn't take long before I'm ready to explode.

Then through clenched teeth, she urges, "Yes, baby. Oooooo! Yes! Fuck me, Rocket."

I pump her faster.

"I've wanted you for so long, Crockett! Go, baby."

Slamming into her sweet little pussy, burying deep and hard, she bounces with the force of my thrusts.

"Hard." She starts to pant.

"Hard!" She pushes me.

"Harder!" Her voice is strained.

I ram back into her, pumping up the pressure, my heartbeat pounding in my ears until the sweet sensation right before ejaculation shuts out all the noise of the world.

"Oh, my God," she screams, then her breath stops.

In that moment is the quiet before the storm when the only sound is pleasure.

My dam breaks. My balls explode. I flex and fuck, jamming into her with short, fast, delicious strokes and snatches of grunts, with the force of an orgasm that wipes clean all memories of any other as I empty my wad as deep as I can inside her.

Her mouth is next to my ear, and her moans of pleasure turn into shocked joyous whimpers as she has another orgasm with me. "OH, OH, OH!"

Drained, I collapse onto her as we gasp for air together. Then I roll off, and my soft cock slips out. We lay staring up at the ceiling side by side, huffing and puffing but happy as hell.

Then she starts to snicker, then giggles, then peals of laughter shake her shoulders.

"What's so fucking funny?" I laugh with her.

"We're so bad! For God's sake, we christened the concession stand counter. They prepare food here!"

I roll onto my side and kiss her lips. "They won't ever know. Besides, it was worth it."

Her big eyes, glistening with tears of laughter, look at me, and the sincerity I see in them rocks my world.

"Yes, it was." Then she sits up and looks around. "Grab the paper towels for me." She points to a roll at the other end. "We made a mess!"

I jump off the counter, pull my pants back up, and do as I'm told. When I hand it to her, I'm grinning. "You look...."

She takes the roll, then holds her hand up, stopping my words. "Anything less than ravishing is the wrong answer."

I chuckle. "How's ravished sound?"

She chuckles with me as she jumps off and wipes our juices running out of her. "That's acceptable."

Putting my shirt back on and stuffing my weapon back into its holster, I take the evidence she hands me and walk over to the trash can to throw it away while she gets dressed.

We walk to the door, and I unlock it, hold my hand out for hers, and interlock our fingers. Pushing the door open, we step outside. At the far end of the field, a man cuts the grass on a riding lawnmower.

We walk back to the fence, grinning. I scoop her up into my arms, and before I set her over the edge, I say, "I feel like I should apologize."

Her eyebrow cocks, "For what?"

"This wasn't exactly the way I envisioned our reunion."

She throws her head back and laughs, "Well, Rocket, it wasn't exactly the way I envisioned it either. It's good." She pecks my nose. "We're good." She looks over the fence, waiting for me to set her over. "You're good."

Standing with the fence between us, she turns to face me. "All eight, nine, ten inches. Just how long is your rocket, anyway?"

God, I do love her in-your-face banter.

Seven

Nina

———

Rocket springs over the fence like a cat then takes my hand again. I cannot believe how high I am flying right now.

Wow! Just wow!

He leads me back across the street, and when we reach the starting point, we stare at each other. "Well?" I ask him.

"Well, what?"

"Are we going to finish this run or not?" I take off, and he comes up beside me, matching my stride. We run the rest of our miles in silence, just enjoying being together again.

When we turn the corner on the home stretch street, we slow down to a walk to cool off. He says, "Okay, time to talk. You go first. Fill me in on your life since I left the team."

She starts off with, "Well, after I cried myself to sleep for a month...." Then she winks, "Life with the team was never the same. I decided not to re-up. I was discharged two weeks ago. I came down here to spend time with my sister's family. I witnessed what happened yesterday. Thank you so much for being you and doing what you do."

He grins that cute grin and says, "So you were the one standing in the shadow at the window?"

I nod. "I was."

"Were you going to hit me up?"

I grin. "Of course."

"When?"

I laugh and bump him as we walk, "Tonight."

"Where?"

"At your bar."

"Hmm." He cuts his eyes at me. "I was going to call you later and offer you a job."

We walk up into the yard and stop.

I tease him, "I guess I'll have to decline the

cushy corporate job I landed that pays above average and has an excellent benefits package and accept your offer. I'm kind of obligated after you saved my niece to join you in the fight."

"You aren't obligated, Foxtrot. You can turn me down. But ..." His eyebrow cocks with his sexy as fuck smirk. "I'm confident I can offer you more."

"I have a pretty sweet deal." I look him up and down. "What are you offering?"

He reaches out and grabs me before I flinch, and pulls me into his arms. Swaying side to side, we tease each other.

"I'm going to need an excellent benefits package."

"I can do that."

"Let's hear it then."

"I'm willing to pay you 20% more than whatever they are offering, and I'll match their employment benefits package." He grins, confident I'll agree.

"Is that it?" I pout.

His hand grips my ponytail, stopping it from swaying with us. He puts just enough tension on it to keep my face in front of his. "Plus, I'll fuck your brains out at the end of every day."

I smile as my eyes close, inhaling his intoxicating musk. "What about the mornings?"

He chuckles, and his warm breath caresses my face. "You're so demanding."

"You have NO idea!" I open my eyes and twinkle at him.

"Mornings too, then, baby." He places a butterfly kiss on my lips.

"Deal." I whisper on his lips, "But I would have worked for free for the plus package."

His eyes crinkle as his lips smile against mine. Then lips capture mine and his tongue slides inside my wanton mouth.

The front door opens, and he reins in his passion, releasing our kiss, and dropping his hands to rest benignly on my waist. Looking over my head, he asks, "How's everyone doing today, ma'am?"

I turn in his arms to see Bri standing on the porch, looking like Christmas came early, "Everyone is good. Thank you."

He nods, looks down at me, and says, "Come to Suds After BUD/S bar when you're done. We can talk there. In private."

"Okay."

He turns and walks a few steps away, then he

stops and turns back. "And pack an overnight bag."

I grin at him as Bri walks up to stand beside me.

She crosses her arms over her chest and asks as we watch him jog away. "Who ... the fuck ... is he?"

"Jeff Crockett. The former team leader of Alpha. We served together in the military."

"My god! And I worried about you all those years. If I had only known...."

I laugh, put my arms around her, and lead her back inside.

She says, "We're going shopping before you go to the bar."

I lean away and frown, "Why?"

"Because I've seen your wardrobe, and you aren't wearing that ratty, conservative shit for him. He deserves corsets, fishnet stockings, and platform stilettos."

I laugh at her. "He's the kind of man that bare ass naked is better."

She snorts, "No, sister! No! A man like that needs to experience the thrill of unwrapping his present every single time." She pushes me through the doorway. "And you are going to blow his mind!"

Crockett

When I get back to my penthouse, I call room service to clean the suite and stock the wet bar with champagne. I want everything perfect with Nina tonight. Then I shower and go down to my office at the back of *Suds After BUD/S*.

With half my focus still on Nina, I start working down my list of ideal team members to hire as Coq Blockers.

The first person I call is Aurelius Moore. The first time I met him he flew support on an Alpha mission. When I ran into him in Vegas a few years back, I discovered he was a wealthy venture capital investor and worth millions. I'm going to need a deep-pocket money man to back Coq Blockers, or it's dead in the water. Running rescue operations will be expensive, and the people who need us won't be able to afford us.

"Hardcore, It's Rocket. How ya been?"

"Good, brother. Are you doing good? I heard you go out and inherited a hotel."

"Yeah, no complaints. Business is good. I'm making a good go of it."

"What's on your mind?"

"Listen, I have an idea for a security business I would like to run by you and get your opinion on."

"Security? Alright. Let's hear it."

I recounted my rescue of Nina's niece and share with him my idea to form a private security company to combat human trafficking.

He isn't hard to convince it's a worthwhile endeavor. Turns out, he and his wife Siri had a scare themselves. last year. He offers, "I'll handle the funding for you myself. Don't worry about money. Send me a list of what you need. Prioritized. Broken down into essentials and wish list."

I laugh, shocked at how easy that was. "You got it."

He asks, "Have you thought about an area for operations, yet?"

"No. You were my first call. You can't hit the target if the weapon isn't loaded."

He laughs, "I think I have a location for you if you don't mind operating on the outskirts of Vegas?"

I smile, "None whatsoever."

"Excellent. There's an old chicken ranch that came on the market a couple of months back. It's out in the middle of nowhere. I've had my eye on it."

"A chicken ranch?"

He chuckles. "Yeah, a whorehouse."

"Oh!" I laugh, "Perfect. I'm calling the company, Coq Blockers."

"Karma, man," he laughs out loud, then asks, "How many acres are you talking about?"

"At least a hundred."

"I may be able to get two."

"Fucking, awesome!"

"Send me that list asap."

"Wilco."

"Out here."

I set the phone down and stare at it, absorbing this isn't a pipe dream now. It's a reality.

Fucking A!

The second call I made is to my former number two, Mike Franks, Mr. Mom. He doesn't even let me finish my sales pitch before he says, "I'm in."

I laugh, "Don't you need to check with the boss first?"

He chuckles. "No, we have four kids now. Two girls and two boys. Toccara will be on board, trust me. Money and getting me out of her hair will be at the top of her why-I-have-to-do-this list."

The third call is to Jack Black, Hammer. "Coq Blockers, Inc? My God! It's perfect! How can I say no to that? Count me in."

The third call is to Jocko Malone. He and his K9 Lucifer were instrumental in the success of more than a few of Alpha team's extractions. A dog will be critical to our success.

As soon as I explain my company and make him an offer, he jumps right on it. "I've married since serving on Alpha, so let me run it by my wife. But I'm confident she will agree. We have two little girls now, and they are my world. I cannot imagine a more rewarding civilian career."

The fourth call I make is to Dirk Sam. He and Hardcore went to flight school together, and he is one hell of a helicopter pilot. His response is the same as the others. "Count me in."

I check the time. It's been two hours. Nina should be rolling in here any minute now.

Fuck, she was gorgeous riding my cock. I shake my head. I need that view again. And again. And again.

I dial Micah Young. He's CIA with superior hacking skills.

"Rocketman, what a great idea. Anytime you need my services, including satellites, just let me know. I'll get you the information you need."

"Alright, man. Thanks. I'll hit you only when I need you."

The last person I touch base with is License to Own. I don't know his real name, but he's a gamer with mad skills. We've been playing first-person shooter games together for years. "License, what's up, man? You streaming?"

"No, I'm just playing, working on my skillset. What's up, Rocket? What can I do for you?"

"Listen, I'm starting a security company, and I'm going to need a UAV operator. You interested?"

"Sure, man. What kind of money are we talking about?"

"The kind that will make you put down your

gaming controller long enough to fly a drone mission."

"Dude, I'm all ears."

I give him the skinny on Coq Blockers, and he says, "It will be an honor to be your overwatch. I'm in."

"Excellent. I'll get up with you. Make me a shopping list."

He whistles. "Now, you're talking!"

Just then, Damien, my bouncer, knocks twice on the door and sticks his head. I whirl the chair around to face him, and he says, "I thought you were waiting for a former team member?"

"I am." I stand up. "Is she here?"

His brow furrows, "Boss, the woman that just walked up to the bar and asked for you is Miss America material."

I grin. "Then she's here. Listen, License. Make a list and forward it to me asap. I gotta go."

"Yes, sir."

Eight

Nina

Leaning against the bar, trying to appear comfortable in the casual corset Bri insisted I buy on our shopping spree this morning and wear to the bar even though it isn't noon yet, her argument was powerful. "Nina, you're setting the foundation of your relationship. Do you want it to be sweats and sneakers? Or corsets and stilettos? Trust me. One will bring you a boring sex life, and one will bring you sugar and spice for life."

When I walked in, the bouncer at the door's

eyes fell immediately on my overflowing tits on full display and gave me a look that made me feel like an escort asking for her Sugar Daddy. I stare at his back as he tells Rocket I am out here waiting for him and smirk. Then he takes a step back, clearing the doorway, and Rocket walks through.

Bri was spot on. The look on his face is priceless, and as he walks over, his SEAL alpha male gait is nothing short of stalking, seductive, and possessive.

Damn! The thrill of knowing that his posturing is for me is a heady feeling and one I intend to get addicted to.

He doesn't stop a polite distance away. He walks right up, invades my personal space, and towers his gorgeous ass over me. His magnetism is so powerful my senses are flooded with his essence, and if I weren't such a badass, I might swoon.

He tips his head, and his body heat hits my exposed, sensitive skin, sending a shiver to my soul. Tiny goosebumps pop out as evidence, and I lick my tingling lips.

He murmurs, "Fuck, Foxtrot. This isn't fair," and the vibration in my ear makes me bite my bottom lip, proof my pussy just soaked itself.

Then his arms wrap around me, pinning mine down, and he jerks me to his body, burying his nose in the nape of my neck and inhaling my scent. "When I let you go, you are going to walk into my office, and I am going to fuck you on my desk. Then we will talk business."

"Wilco," I whisper, and his primal growl responds.

He sets me free, and without looking at him or around the room, I strut my corseted badass to his office, understanding escorts in a new and respectful way.

When I walk in, I take note of the decor. His desk sits in front of a single-pane picture window with a spectacular view. It gives a sense of openness, but it has complete privacy because we're on the top floor. The furniture is very masculine, heavy, dark wood. The walls are covered with candid pictures from his military days. He and his Alpha brothers laughing, shooting hoops, or grappling.

I walk over to the wall as he closes the door. The lock clicks as I stop and stare at a picture of me and him, arm and arm, smiling, happy. He walks up behind me and slips his arms around me. I lean against him and confess, "I remember when this was taken."

He doesn't say anything, and I continue. "It was after my first op with Alpha. You were going around congratulating the team, and when you came to me, I was scared shitless."

His arms squeeze my waist.

"And I was right to be. As soon as you touched me, I knew." I spin around to face him. "The fucking fireworks were there."

His cocky smirk teases his sculpted lips. He is so damn good-looking. I drop my eyes to his chest and take his tie between my fingers. I tug gently as I look at him from under my lashes and continue my confession. "I saw it in your eyes. You knew what you did to me. You felt it too."

He grins, "I won't lie. It was hard as fuck treating you like one of the guys when you were so obviously not."

I smirk. "Well, thank you for keeping your hands off me. Working with Alpha was an honor."

He smiles at me. "My team had no idea the sacrifice I made every goddamn day for them."

He leans down to kiss me, but I put my finger on his lips.

"It doesn't matter now, but I do want to know why you didn't contact me after you got out. I hoped you would, and quite frankly, I was heartbroken when you didn't. Your silence made me doubt this." I wag my index finger back and forth between us.

He frowns, studies my face, then reaches up and tucks a stray strand of hair behind my ear. It's such an intimate, caring action my heart melts, and no matter what he says, it really doesn't matter. I was right all along. We do have a chemical connection, and I know Crockett. I know him better than I know my own sister. We have been through so much shit together. Real shit. Shit that matters—life and death shit. And what I know is Jeff Crockett is a man of honor and integrity to his core. Whatever the reason, he made the best decision given the choices before him at the time.

"Foxtrot, you know me. You know I'm not a man that accepts half-ass commitment." His voice is husky with emotion. "I thought about it, but the reason was the same. You needed to be focused on Alpha, not me."

His loyalty is irreproachable. Always willing to do whatever it took for his team, even at the expense of his own happiness.

I slip my hand behind his head and pull his mouth down to consume mine. I whisper right before our lips touch, "Loving you will be all-consuming for me?"

His whispered, "yes," sets me on fire.

At first, his kiss is tender and loving, and I cherish being cherished, but then his lips leave mine and travel down my neck. The lower he goes, the more demanding his mouth becomes and the more consumed I am.

I want his body like his heart right now. Naked. Exposed. Bare.

My fingers claw his shirt out of his suit pants, and he releases me, kicking off his shoes as he removes his tie. Then our hands work together as a team, unbuttoning his shirt. He lets it slide down his arms to the floor as I run my hands down his trousers the length of his hidden hard-on. He is a good eight to ten inches.

As he slides the zipper down, I drop to my knees and wait. Staring up at him, I admire his perfect body as I prepare to worship him properly.

He leans forward, and as his huge chest approaches, I see the scars he received from his Trident pinning ceremony the day he officially became a Navy SEAL. His big, strong arms flex as he pushes the slacks off his ass. His chiseled abs ripple as he straightens back up, and his molded 'v' points to his pumped erection between his tree-trunk legs.

As soon as his cock is free, I reach for it, open my mouth wide, and slide it inside. He's too long to take it all, but I love what I can. My eyes close with the satisfaction of finally tasting him after all these years.

His hands rest on my head, and his fingers flex in my hair as I slobber and suck him. He groans, then latches onto my hair. Stopping my motion. He pulls me to my feet. His eyes are closed, so I stare at his beautiful mouth as it says, "Not yet, Nina."

My God. I nearly swoon. He has never called me Nina. Always Foxtrot. The way his deep voice vibrated as he hummed the 'n' sound is a turn-on I never expected. It is the same pitch as the primal growl he makes that is sexy as fuck but hearing it as he says my name is fucking sexy as fucking fuck!

I turn around and poke my ass out as I lean over. Reaching behind, I unzip my black leather skirt. It falls to the ground, and the view I give him is my bare ass, garter belt, and black thigh-high stockings with little red bows that match my red stiletto heels.

The "umm, fuck me" that oozes from his mouth with the same primal throat hum fuels my fantasy. I have had fuck buddies before, but we only had friend sex, and although Rocket is a closer friend than any of them were, this sex between us is not that kind of fucking.

This is serious sex. This sex means something. This sex is the kind of sex where pleasing your partner is more important than pleasing yourself, but you know you will be pleasured beyond your wildest expectations.

This is making love!

I reach behind, grab my ass cheeks, and pull them apart.

He moans and says, "Your pussy is pure perfection." Then he steps up, hooks my hips, and eases his cock inside.

A low moan slips out of my mouth, and my knees get weak with the pleasure from his stroke. Both his hands grasp my hips, and he thrusts deep inside. My hands shoot straight out to brace against the wall, and he fucks me from behind under the first picture ever taken of us.

With every deep thrust, he lifts my weight off my heels, rocking me forward, and I can't stop the soft whimper of pleasure I emit when he hits that sweet spot no one, not even my vibrator, has struck before. He pauses, and my pussy throbs, aching with need, then he grunts, and his spurt of cum hits that sweet spot, and I lose my shit. My orgasm starts. My legs stiffen and quiver uncontrollably. He hammers it home, deep, and another spurt nails that spot. My head drops as the quivering intensifies. The sensation *is* all-consuming. The only thing that exists at this moment in time is his cock loving my pussy. He grunts as he finishes fast and furious, and I come unglued with the most intense, hard, long, exquisite orgasm I have ever had seizes my body, and I squirt with contractions.

When we are done, we collapse to the floor. Exhausted but exhilarated. He leans his back against the wall and pulls me into his lap. I cuddle with him until my pounding blood slows back to normal.

NINE

Crockett

―――

I PULL NINA INTO MY ARMS AND ENJOY THE afterglow of making wild, passionate, leave-your-inhibitions-at-the-door sex with someone I love. She was confident and fierce in her duties as targeting officer for Alpha, and she is just as secure and fierce in sex.

Fucking A! The first half of my life was filled with heroic warrior moments. The last half will be filled with an epic all-consuming love. Not a bad life.

She lays her face on my chest, and I play with

a garter strap as we recuperate. After a few minutes, I kiss her hair, "Hey, you need to get up."

"Mmm, I like listening to your heartbeat." She says and doesn't move.

"I like you listening to it too, but my legs are going to sleep."

"Oh," she says, then she places a great big wet smooch on my lips before she stands. She looks around the room, "Paper towels?"

"At the bar, but theirs a bathroom behind that door."

She flashes a bright smile and heads that way. I marvel at how the time that separated us seems to have vanished. We picked right up where we left off, but with one significant difference.

I walk to the bar for the paper towels to clean the puddle. *Best sex ever!*

When she returns, the room is clean, and I'm sitting in the overstuffed chair, putting on my shoes. She walks over to stand in front of me. I lean back in the chair and lift my face to her. She grins, looking down at me. Her hourglass shape is more pronounced with the extra weight, and she is absolutely gorgeous.

She puts her knee on the chair, then straddles

me, sitting on my lap. As she begins to button my shirt, I ask, "Do you always go commando?"

She grins, "Most of the time. Why?"

I close my eyes, enjoying her fingers tickling my skin as they work on the buttons. "I'm just thankful I didn't know that back then."

She giggles, "I'm thankful you know it now."

I grin as I slide my hands over the soft, smooth skin of her ass. "Are you hungry?"

"Starving."

She orders a cheeseburger, rare with loaded fries, and a beer. I order a steak, medium-rare with broccoli, rice, and water. While we eat, we catch up on what's what, and I learn her sister, Bri, is a widow and her niece, Bethany, is her only child. "They will be forever grateful to you for stepping up and saving her. To us, rescuing her was a no-brainer. But to them, only heroes step up."

"You can thank me later for them." I wink, and she laughs. "What about your personal life? Any men I need to be aware of?"

"Just one. It ended badly. At first, he was

charming and considerate. But then he became abusive."

"How abusive?" The hair on my neck stands on end.

Her eyebrow cocks in that familiar 'no bullshit allowed' way she has. "He had the audacity to try to take what I wasn't offering."

I put my hand up, "Do I need to hear this? Cause I'll get fired up."

She laughs and says, "Yes, you do. You need to know if I say no for whatever reason, no means fucking no."

I cut my eyes at her. "Are you serious right now?"

"Yes, I'm serious."

"Do you honestly think I wouldn't stop if you said no?"

Her eyes soften, and I see regret. "No, Rocket, I don't honestly think that. I know you would."

"But he didn't."

She shakes her head. "No, he didn't. He tried to rape me."

The pit of my gut knots, and I feel my lips compress into a hard line. I shake my head. "Tried?"

"Yes," She smiles and leans forward to kiss my forehead. "He tried, so I fucked him up."

"Explain how you fucked him up because if it doesn't meet my approval, I'm going to plan a midnight raid."

"I tased his nuts."

"Damn," I snort. "That *is* fucking him up."

Her eyebrow cocks again, "He literally crawled out of my place, and I never heard from him again."

I laugh, "So, no, is your safe word?"

She grins, "Correct. No is my safe word."

I pucker my lips and kiss hers. "Copy that."

When I let her go, she asks, "What about you? What have you been doing since Alpha?"

I smirk, "Look around, babe. Getting this place profitable again has been my life. Between the hotel, the restaurant, and the bar, I haven't had time for much of anything else. I eat, sleep, and work."

"Speaking of work," She grins, "Let's discuss my new position with your new company."

"You're my first official hire."

"Oh! Well, we are ground zero then." She grins, making me laugh.

"Yes, Foxtrot, we are ground zero."

I show her my notes, and we discuss the ins and outs of running a private company like a military operation. I explain how the money will flow and how we will utilize my CIA and gaming connections to fill in the overwatch positions. I give her the list of SEALs that have agreed to join us, and she agrees we have a good group of guys.

"But there is so much to do." She looks at me with her big eyes.

"It's a huge undertaking." I nod in agreement, "but one worth doing."

"Oh, absolutely! I'll have nightmares for the rest of my life about what almost happened to Bethany, knowing it happens every day to innocent children. But we'll be there for at least some of them. Thank you for including me."

She leans forward for a kiss, and I slip my hand around the nape of her neck and shove my tongue into her willing mouth.

TEN
PART TWO

Las Vegas, NV
MAY 16, 2010

———

Aurelius Moore
Chief Financial Officer

I DRIVE THE JAGUAR UNDER THE CANOPY AT Been Jammin's Gentleman's Club and stop.

Siri leans toward me for a peck. "Have a good day, Aurei. I can't wait to hear how everything is progressing."

"I'll give you a full report before we fall asleep tonight." I peck her perfectly puckered lips. "Bring down the house tonight, Wild Thang."

Her door opens as Jimmy reaches in for her hand, "Mrs. Moore."

She takes his hand, swings her legs onto the concrete, and stands, saying, "Jimmy, you are such a gentleman."

"Morning, Sir." He leans in and says, "I'll escort her to her dressing room personally."

I thank him as he closes the door. Then I ease out of the parking lot.

But as soon as I hit the on-ramp, I peg the speedometer needle into the dashboard and scream down the freeway at 100 plus miles per hour. Excited to see what improvements have been made to the chicken ranch.

As I drive down the property line, I note the obvious improvements. There is a new security fence that extends as far as the eye can see, encompassing the entire property.

When I turn off the road and enter the private drive, I note the original big wooden overhead sign spanning the driveway that reads, Welcome to The Chicken Ranch, has a brand new company logo swinging underneath it.

I stop at the security gate and spool down my window, getting a kick out of the sign hanging from the fortified heavy gate. "Trespassers will be shot on sight and buried before anyone knows you're missing."

A female's voice says, "State your name."

"Aurelius Moore," I answer.

"State your business."

"Property inspection," I smirk.

"Do you have an appointment?"

"No, I have an invitation."

"Standby."

I wait only a few seconds before the gate retreats enough for me to enter the compound.

When I top the hill, the original ranch buildings come into view. All have been updated with fresh paint. The ranch house is welcoming.

A new asphalt parking lot was poured on the side and three cars and one truck are parked there. A good walking distance away is the bunkhouse. Its parking lot is full of trucks, jeeps, and motorcycles. I smirk, Team parking.

The barn is busy with activity, and a cowboy leads two horses out to be saddled.

I pull in and park next to a black Ford Bronco with vinyl signage on the side panel that matches the hanging sign at the entrance. The company name is Coq Blockers, and I chuckle again that Rocket named his company that.

When I step out of my jag, I hear my name, "Hardcore! Come on in. We'll start the tour in here."

The layout is a big spacious parlor and in the center sits a chic welcome center with a corporate receptionist who smiles and stands to greet us.

Surrounding her are areas sectioned off by the strategic placement of household furniture. Couches, chairs, recliners, TV's, video game stations, and an array of toy boxes for different age groups of children.

Crockett enters the room with his hand outstretched. "Well, what do you think so far?"

I smirk and nod, "I like it. It almost looks like you've entered a family's home."

He grins and pumps my hand. "That's the idea. We want to offer our customers a place where they feel safe during their crisis."

He introduces me to the young woman standing. "I'd like you to meet Meghan Meadows. She's the first person our customers will meet. We call her the Ambassador."

I nod, and she winks at me. "My job is to keep everyone calm."

I reach for her outstretched hand and shake it. Her long auburn hair is neatly tied back in a braid. Her coloring suggests she has Irish blood. Her smile is pleasant and genuine.

"Nice to meet you, sir." She says, "Rocket speaks very highly of you."

Jeff continues, "Meghan is former ISR, Air Force Intelligence, Surveillance, and Reconnaissance. She will screen the requests we receive and handle the investigative portion of the hunt."

We follow Meghan into the dining room, and Crockett continues the tour. "The entire upstairs floor consists of bedrooms that will house our customers if need be."

We enter the original kitchen area, and he continues, "The kitchen is fully functional. The staff arrived yesterday and will serve the personnel their first meal tonight. You are welcome to join us."

I nod and take a bottle of water from Meghan. "Not tonight. Thanks. Siri is performing her last show and I promised to catch it. We're flying home afterward for a much-needed break."

Meghan asks, "So your wife is a performer?"

I nod. "Yes, she's the headlining star of Been Jammin' Gentleman's Club."

Her eyebrows raise like everyone's does, so I explain further.

"She's a performer, not a stripper. Although she started out as a stripper, and her costumes don't leave much to the imagination."

Jeff chuckles, "I gotta hand it to you, Hardcore, you're a bigger man than me."

I smirk, "What she does now is tame to what she used to do."

He nods, "I really need to catch a show."

"I can get you tickets when she returns." I look at Meghan. "Would you like tickets as well?"

"Oh! Wow! Absolutely! Thank you!"

I nod as Crockett leads the way back to the parlor. When we enter, he points to the door he is walking toward, "The Family Command Center is through here."

He opens the door, then stops in the doorway. "Ambassador, let's put identifying signs on the doors. Small, tactful."

She responds, "Copy that."

He continues inside, and I follow, "We will give the families briefings here during the mission. One in the morning and one in the evening. Once the mission is accomplished, they will receive an after-action debriefing with instructions on where they will be reunited with their loved one."

I look around the room. There is a large table in the center. Along the walls are a giant video screen and candid photos of the team members when they served as special warfare operators.

It is a nice touch, designed to instill confidence in the teams' ability to run a successful rescue mission without bragging. Something Navy SEALS never do.

"Ready to see the Coq Coop?"

I laugh, "Lead the way."

We walk back to Meghan's desk, then out the

front door. He heads toward the barn, not his truck, so I ask, "What are we taking to the Coop?"

Crockett laughs, "Horses. They need riding."

"Hang on, then." I jog over to the jag, pop the trunk, and pull out my cowboy hat and boots.

Crockett laughs, "I didn't take you for a cowboy."

I grin, "I'm a man with many secrets."

He laughs. "Copy that."

Eleven

Crockett

———

I introduce Hardcore to the cowboys at the barn that will manage the stables. The head ranch hand is Theo, and they discuss how transporting the horses to different locations should be handled.

Hardcore tells Theo to check into renting a special cargo plane to transport them when necessary. "We want the details locked in and ready to roll. When shit happens, it happens fast, and minutes count. Details matter. If the horses are needed, we'll need to move them quickly."

Theo nods, and when he looks at me, he gives me a wink that says Hardcore is a-okay in his book.

Hardcore looks at me, then looks at the horses saddled. "Which one do you want?"

I laugh. "Based on your boots, hat, and your convo with Theo, I want the old tame mare, not that young stud. He's all yours."

He chuckles, takes the reins, strokes the horse's mane at his ears, and speaks to him. "We're not going to have any trouble, are we, big guy?"

He pats him hard on the neck twice, then he steps to the saddle, places the reins on the horn, puts his foot in the stirrup, and pulls himself up. The horse dances away before he can swing his leg over. I hear his deep voice speaking calmly, "Whoa, boy. Easy now. Let me get in the saddle before you bolt, please." Then he swings his leg over, sets his ass firmly in the saddle, and pulls the reins tight. The horse responds by bobbing his head, trying to gain slack on the bit in his mouth, but Hardcore pulls him into a fast left turn and tells me, "Mount up, man. This guy needs to run."

I swing myself into the saddle and

comfortably sit on the much tamer mare, then I give a little kick, and we are off. Hardcore gives the stud his head and lets him run. While I gallop smoothly after him.

When Hardcore circles back, I slow down and walk so we can talk. He pulls alongside me.

I chuckle. "That one has a lot of attitude."

"Ah. He's good. He needs a firm hand. Who is your most experienced rider?"

"Hammer. He's a Texan."

He nods. "Are we going the right way? I forgot to ask which direction."

We laugh, and I point in front of us. "Yes, we will check out the firing range first, then the obstacle course. Visit the warehouse where the target models will be constructed, then meet up with the team members still here to tour the Coop. They have spent the last two weeks on-site training, and I believe we are ready to roll."

He nods, and we ride in silence for a bit, but then he asks, "How many operators do you have?"

"Four, which we can go with, but I lack two for a complete team."

"Who are they?"

"The two men you will meet today were my

number two and three from Alpha. Mike Franks, Mr. Mom, and Jack Black, Hammer, he likes to blow shit up."

He laughs.

"Jocko Malone. I believe you know him already."

"Know of him. We haven't met yet. Siri's scheduled Angel's final security guard training with him and his K9."

He nods. "You won't be disappointed. Lucifer is an amazing MPC [multipurpose canine]."

He nods, then asks, "Weapons?"

"Got 'em."

"NVG's [night vision goggles]?"

I laugh, "Hard, we're ready."

He laughs too. "I've been in the civilian world too long."

I chuckle. "I understand. I had difficulty adjusting to the civilian work ethic when I took over the hotel."

He laughs. "There is no substitute for follow-up."

I laugh. "Times five."

He chuckles, too, kicks his horse, and takes off again, letting his horse run circles around me.

When we arrive at the firing range, I pull my

horse to a stop, shift my ass in the saddle, and wait for Hardcore to pull up next to me. He asks, "So, what are we looking at here?"

I point in the direction of a group of trees on a small hill. "Those trees are a mile away. That's the farthest target."

"That's a hell of a shot to make. Who's the sniper?"

I grin, "You're looking at him."

He gives me a head nod.

I point out the other targets and explain. "They are calibrated to match a man running." I wheel my horse away. "The obstacle course is next."

When we arrive, the first thing he says is, "I'm coming out here to work out with y'all. This looks like fun."

I laugh. "You are welcome anytime, but don't expect to win."

He laughs too.

We dismount, tie the horses up in the shade, and go inside the warehouse. There is a model of a house built with just the walls, no roof, and a viewing tower built around the top of the warehouse walls. I head for the stairs and take two at a time to the top. When I step onto the landing, Hardcore is right behind me. We stroll out onto the viewing platform, and I explain how we will use the maze to train breaching, entering, snatching, and retrieving our targets under a time limit. "Like you said earlier, 'Minutes count. Details matter.'"

"Yes, they do."

As we trot down the stairs, Hardcore says, "I tell ya, Crockett, I'm impressed so far."

I laugh, "Then be prepared to have your mind blown because I saved the best for last."

When we enter The Coop, it feels like returning to Alpha. Mike, Jack, and Nina all stand when they see Aurelius is with me. I introduce each of the guys, they shake hands, then I turn to Nina. I lift my arm, and she slides underneath it.

"And this is my main squeeze, Nina Fox, Foxtrot. She was the targeting officer for Alpha, and for Coq Blockers, she'll be the mission commander as well."

She pats me on the chest and cocks that damn eyebrow. "Main squeeze? I better be the only damn squeeze."

Everyone laughs.

Then she steps forward and shakes

Hardcore's hand. "Nice to meet the man whose money I have spent so freely."

Everyone laughs again.

"Nice to meet the woman who took his idea and has made it a reality."

She nods, pleased with the compliment. "Let me share with you what you purchased and how we will use it."

They walk across the room to the three video screens along the far wall, and I pull up a chair to sit at the conference table with Mike and Jack.

As they go, she talks animatedly about the surveillance items she has purchased and their purposes. She is wearing a gray T-shirt that is too tight across her breasts with black yoga pants and flip-flops. Her hair is hanging straight, and I love how it swings as she moves. She rarely wears makeup, and I prefer her natural beauty most of the time. But at night, when she dresses up just for me ... *Mmhmm.*

Hardcore asks her some questions, and she answers by escorting him to the back. In the adjoining room are individual cages that house our personal shit, and beyond that is the warehouse where the equipment she bought is housed.

Mike laughs when we hear the door close. "Foxtrot is in her element now. Let's give her ten minutes, then one of us needs to go rescue him."

Jack laughs, "Hell, no. He's the one that gave her a blank check. He needs to see all the shit she bought."

I laugh. "Hardcore can take care of himself. I'm not going in there and interrupting her."

Forty minutes later, Nina and Aurelius walk back in and find us cleaning our weapons. I have an M240 machine gun, while Mike and Jack both have MP7 machine pistols, broken down and scattered on the table.

Jack jokes, "Did you get to see every single thing she's bought?"

Aurelius laughs as Nina sasses him, "When your ass is on a mission, and that equipment saves your hairy hide, you'll be thanking me for making sure you had the best."

Mike pushes his chair back, "Oh, snap!"

Hardcore leans forward and pretends to whisper, "She even showed me the parachutes."

Jack gives him a knuckle bump, and everyone laughs, including Nina.

Mike asks, "How about we give him an aerial tour?"

I slap him on the back, "Mom, that is an excellent idea! Go get the UAV [unmanned aerial vehicle] ready, and I'll get License on the Manpack radio."

Nina lays her phone on the table, swipes to the stopwatch, and says, "Go."

Mike and Jack both stand up, and their chairs nearly flip over in their rush to beat the clock. Nina and I walk over to the command station. She turns on the video screen while I cue up License.

He answers, "License to Own is mission-ready, Rocket."

I smile and respond. "Standby for activation."

We turn to look at the grey snow on the video screen, then all of a sudden, Hammer's face is talking to us. "Which one of you rode Demon?"

I key the handset. "Hardcore."

His laughing face retreats on the screen, "Nothing like breaking in the FNG [fucking new guy]."

Mike's voice says, "Crank her up, License."

The hum of the drone comes over the radio, and Mike says, "Airborne."

Nina hits the stopwatch and says, "Three minutes, twenty seconds."

On the screen, we see a clear picture of the outside with Mike and Jack standing up looking at it. Then we see them being targeted and high tailing it back inside.

The door opens, and they rush in.

"What the fuck, License?" Mike keys his handset, but License doesn't respond. He's on radio silence.

He gives us an aerial tour of the ranch and puts the drone through multiple maneuvers. Demonstrating how effective the camera is at high altitude and how stealthy it can be in the woods.

When he flies it over the Ranch House, he explains that it is not only night vision capable but has thermal imaging capabilities. He flips it on, and we see Meghan's heat signature sitting at the desk.

Nina tells Hardcore, "So once the satellite has identified the target, overwatch can maintain surveillance while the calvary is called in for the rescue."

"Excellent demonstration, License. Bring her in."

"Roger. Wilco, Rocket."

Mike and Jack go back out the door, and we hear Mike telling License over the handset as the drone flies back to The Coop. "You know what our call names are, don't you, License?"

"Yeah, Mom and Hammer."

"That's right, Boot. And if you pull that stunt again, you're going to find out why."

The radio goes silent, and we watch the drone fly in. Then we hear License, "Requesting permission for a flyby."

I key the radio. "That's a negative, License."

But we hear, "Sorry, Rocket, but buzzing the tower is gonna happen."

As the drone climbs, we watch on the screen, as it goes into a hard dive, gathering speed, flying low over the building, then shooting out over the area where Mike and Jack stand waiting and coming to an abrupt stop. Finally settling, nice and slow, at their feet.

Mike keys the radio. "Perfect landing, License."

He laughs on the other end. "Game over. License To Own out here."

I announce, "And that, Ladies and

Gentlemen, concludes today's demonstration. Coq Blockers is mission ready."

"Impressive." Hardcore stands and says to Nina, "You've done a fantastic job getting them ready to roll."

She smiles, "Thank you."

Meghan keys the radio. "Chow time, boys."

I respond. "On the way. We will hitch a ride back to the Ranch House with Foxtrot. Mom and Hammer can ride the horses back."

Twelve

Nina

I flip on the lights as I enter my apartment. Rocket is right behind me. "Want a glass of wine?" He asks as he walks toward the kitchen.

"No, thanks," I call over my shoulder, making my way through the living room, heading for the bedroom. When I flip on the light, I ask him, "Do you have a preference for tonight?" But he doesn't answer, so I open my closet and stare at my clothes, trying to decide whether to dress down with comfy skinny jeans or dress up in a sexy dress, or a mixture of both. I haven't worn the corset since day one. Maybe I will wear that.

Tuned into where he is, I hear the refrigerator door open and the clink of glass on glass as he removes a cold one. Then the door closes, the top comes off the bottle and lands in the garbage can.

Free to tease, taunt, and flirt now, I want his eyes hungry, needy, horny when they look at me. Not just tonight, but every single time.

I hear the beer bottle land in the garbage can, and I turn toward him, sensing he is getting closer. He stops in the doorway to stare.

I grin. "What do you prefer I wear tonight?"

He smirks that cute 'devil be damned' look, and that killer dimple flashes me. My pussy constricts, and my heart melts. "Fuck! Rocket, don't do that."

"Do what?" He feigns innocence.

"That!" I point my finger at him and wave it around the air, indicating from head to toe his gorgeousness. "I don't want to miss the show."

He laughs, teasing me with his eyes. "We have an hour and a half before the curtain goes up. That's plenty of time for my rocket to send you into orbit."

I laugh, "You do know how corny that is, don't you?"

He chuckles as he strips, slowly peeling off every stitch of clothing, and I forget everything but watching him unveil his massive, muscular frame.

Crockett is six-foot-five and weighs in at a trim two hundred and sixty pounds. His dark blonde looks fit the 'All American Man' type with hawkish brown eyes flecked with gold; angled brows; longer than scuff length beard; straight hair cropped close on the side that's long and full on top with sandy highlights; a hard firm jaw; straight nose; sculpted, full lips on an athletic body that could play any professional sport.

He is a man that stands out in a crowd. Whether he is wearing fatigues and combat boots or a business suit and tie, he is a stud that oozes hero, and I worship the ground the man walks on.

When he is completely naked, he strolls over to me, slides his strong hands over the sensitive skin of my neck, cups my face, and tilts it up to stare helplessly yet emboldened to do whatever he asks of me. He whispers, "You know I prefer you naked."

I smile, "I do."

His hands release my face, but I remain locked on him. My eyes feeding on his hunger for me. I feel the tips of his finger as they find the hem of my shirt and grasp it. Then the soft fabric stimulates my skin as he lifts it. I close my eyes only long enough for the fabric to clear my face, then lock onto his love again.

He smiles a soft, gentle smile and tells me he loves me without saying a word.

His lips touch mine, and the sweet sensations of loving him and being loved by him soar through me. My soul sings with happiness. His kiss moves from my mouth down my neck. His fingers find the latch of my bra and squeeze the ends together. The hooks unbound, the strap pops off, and my tits dangle free. Waiting for his mouth's arrival, they harden with anticipation. His kisses linger on my neck as he pushes the straps off my shoulders, and my bra falls to the ground.

I sigh, lost in his touch, found in his love making. Life has never been more fulfilling than this. Crockett is my world. My everything.

His lips kiss their way down to my breasts, and my head falls back with sweet surrender. My mind saturated with pleasure as his thumbs hook the waistband of my yoga pants and push them down off my ass.

My skin is so tuned in, waiting for his touch, that tiny goosebumps breakout when the air blows over the exposed area. He moans that throat moan when he tastes the ripple of the goosebumps.

"God, I love how your body responds to me." He whispers as he kisses his way down, pushing the soft fabric to my ankles.

His tongue passes over my clit as he inserts it, tasting my wetness, and I jerk from the jolt of pure pleasure. Grabbing his head, I wrap my fingers in his hair to steady myself as he licks while lifting my feet free of the fabric.

By the time I am naked, my pussy throbs for penetration, and my whole being yearns for his possession. In the short time that it takes him to stand, I nearly collapse with need.

His deep moan acknowledges his power over me as his strong arms wrap themselves around me and lifts me off my feet. I spread my legs wide for him, opening the gateway to my soul. His cock, big, bold, beautiful, slides inside, and we become one.

Free of any constraints, we fuck until we explode together with passion.

Then I collapse on him, and he cuddles me, holding me tight while we recuperate.

After a few moments, I lift my face, kiss his chest, and say, "I think I saw stars."

He chuckles as he slowly lowers me down to stand on my own feet. "I told you my rocket was going to send you into orbit."

I laugh too. "Yes, you did."

When we arrive at Been Jammin', we walk through the casino to the Whitney Houston's, I Will Always Love You, Cirque du Soleil show ticket counter and get in line. There are five couples in front of us, so it moves fast, and we are seated well before the show starts.

The auditorium surrounds the stage on three sides, and there are hundreds of seats. We are in the middle at eye level. Crockett's broad chest is wider than the seat, so he puts his arm around the back of mine and leans over to give the woman sitting next to him her space. I cuddle up under his wing, and his fingertips play against my skin where they touch. "Comfy?"

I nod, "and cozy."

He chuckles.

The lights dim, and the show begins. For the next two hours, we watch a beautiful blonde woman transform herself in and out of the personification of the late, great Whitney Houston.

Siri sings with a voice that so closely matches Whitney's that at first, I thought she was lip syncing, only to be proven wrong when she added a spoken word tribute to her. The production consists of silhouettes and slide shows across Whitney's mega screen, while Siri dances either solo or as a group with other dancers. The routines vary based on the song, but each is unique, different, and wonderful!

It is by far the best live show I have ever seen, and when Crockett drives us home, I ask him. "Is Siri not phenomenal?"

"She is pretty amazing."

"I keep trying to decide which song was my favorite."

"Why?" He cuts his eyes at me.

"Why, what?" I frown at him.

"Why choose a favorite?"

"I don't know. But I think it's a toss-up between 'I Wanna Dance with Somebody' and 'I Will Always Love You.'"

"Why?" He cuts his eyes again.

I smirk at him. "You're messing with me, aren't you?"

He grins, "I just want to learn what makes you tick, babe."

I grin, "Thank God, I never realized how sweet you are."

He chuckles, "Why?"

I laugh out loud. "Because I would have broken all the rules just to be with you."

His smile is dream-worthy, and I continue letting him get closer to me. "The way Siri danced around the group of other dancers with 'I Wanna Dance with Somebody' was fun to watch. It was great! Her energy, her vibe, totally fun! You know if you went out with her for drinks, you would have a blast."

He interrupts, "When."

I frown, "When, what?"

"When you go out with drinks with her."

I grin, "My God, that's right! She is hitched to Hardcore."

He nods.

"How cool is that?" I totally fangirl on him.

He chuckles, "What's the other favorite song?"

"The finale, of course," I turn to face him in the seat. My knee props on the center console, and his hand drops off the steering wheel to rest on it. The simple move is so intimate, my heart fills with love for him. "That song pulls at your heartstrings anyway, but when Siri walked out singing it, looking exactly like Whitney, I was blown away. I showed you the goosebumps that popped out. It was unforgettable."

He smiles as his thumb strokes my skin.

"I had a blast!" I tell him, "Thanks for taking me."

He cuts his eyes at me, and a little scowl rests on his brow. He says, "Of course."

God, I love this man!

Thirteen
Part Three

San Diego, California
June 1, 2010

Crockett

The sun is setting when I walk into the Hotel. The twins are sitting in the lobby area. As soon as they spot me, they stand and head my way.

They haven't been around in months. They

aren't aware I've hooked up with Nina. I stop and wait to greet them.

Although I call them the twins, they aren't related. They are best friends that I have had a fucking relationship with for years. Nothing personal. Just sex.

They are all smiles as they slink over. They look good. They are wearing matching, barely-cover-your-ass, daringly-low-tease-you-with-my-tits, figure-forming, paint-the-town-red, sparkling, nightclub dresses. One is royal blue; the other is lime green. Their dyed, platinum-blonde hair and tanning bed bronze skin is accentuated by the bright colors.

"Evening, double trouble." I lean over so they can peck my cheeks. "Looking beautiful as always tonight. Heading up to the bar or going to catch The Lost Boys Dinner Show?"

"We thought we would head up to the bar. There's a convention of lawyers partying."

Nina walks up with Mike and Jack, followed by Jocko with Lucifer on a leash, and Dirk. We're assembling here tonight before Dirk flies us to Vegas in the morning. We have a week of training scheduled at The Chicken Ranch for parachute jumps and repelling from the helicopter.

Remembering her comment earlier, I introduce Nina and make sure the twins understand that she is my *only* squeeze. To their credit, the twins don't bat an eye at the news, and thankfully, Nina remains clueless about our prior fucking arrangement. Before the introductions are over, they are sizing up the guys.

I run through them quickly. "Men, these are the twins. Twins, Mike, Jack, Jocko, and Dirk. The twins are literally salivating, and Mike defends himself first.

Throwing his hands up, he says, "Don't even. I'm married with four kids."

Jocko's next, "I've got two."

Dirk says, "I've got zero, but I'm hitched to a crazy Brit." He puts his arm around Jack and shoves him forward. "Here's your man, right here."

Jack sticks his elbows out and says, "Ladies, Hammer at your service."

They pull his massive arms tight against their boobs, and the new threesome heads to the elevator without a backward glance at us.

I look down at Nina to see her smirk is severe. I ask, "What?"

She shakes her head and rolls her eyes. So

much for being clueless. I smirk back at her. "What can I say?"

"Nothing." Mike chimes in. "Don't say a fucking word. It's a trap."

Dirk adds, "Best advice ever, bro. Keep your damn mouth shut, and you won't stick your foot in it nearly as much."

Nina hooks my arm pulls it into her tits, and says, "Come on, Rocket, I need a shower and a party dress if that's the competition."

Just then, my phone rings. She rolls her eyes and waves as she takes off for my private elevator. "I'll meet you guys there."

The guys laugh at her as I answer. "Crockett, here."

"Crockett, it's Brody. I am in town for the weekend, and I need a room. Can you hook me up?"

My gears begin to grind. "No problem, B. A. You can stay as long as you like."

Brody Andrews wasn't on my list, but only because he's still active duty. He and I go way back. When he was deciding to become a SEAL or not, we talked about it. Timing is everything. He would be a good fit with this tight group.

"Thanks, brother. I need you to do me a favor too. A couple of them, actually."

I grin. He is going to owe me then. "Just ask. You know I'll do whatever I can."

"I need you to put me in a room as close to Lizzy Mayer's as possible, and I need a ticket to the dinner show."

I chuckle and head over to Linda at the reservation counter. "Does Miss Mayer, or is it Mrs., have a ticket to the dinner show too?"

He laughs, "It is Miss, and yes, she does."

"Standby," I tell him.

Then I give Linda the details on the room and dinner show, and she begins clicking away on the keyboard.

"Make sure the kitchen knows to give him extra portions of the dinner meal and that his drinks are on me. Give him a VIP pass for Suds too."

She smiles. "Yes, sir." After a few moments, she gives me the room information and prints his dinner show ticket.

I tell Brody, "All set. You're in the room next to hers and sitting at her table for the show. The show starts in an hour. How far out are you?"

"Fifteen, if I don't get stuck in traffic."

"We'll catch up on your unit later then. Your ticket will be waiting for you at the door along with a VIP pass for Suds. Drinks are on me."

"You're too good to me. Thanks."

"Looking forward to your mission recap. I want all the sick details! Crockett, out here." I disconnect the call and walk back over to the guys. "Let's go get a beer and a bite to eat. There will be a table on the deck waiting for us."

"Hooyah."

When we step off the elevator, the noise confirms tonight will be profitable. The guys head on in while I search for Damien. He has taken up his bouncer post at the entrance in front of the public elevator. Scanning the crowd, always ready for trouble.

He is a former SEAL too, and although I asked him to join Coq Blockers, he declined. "I'm good being your bodyguard, bartender, and bouncer, Rocket. If you get in a bind, I won't say no to running an op, but I prefer to spend my nights wrapped in the arms of my woman."

I patted his arm and said, "You'll be the first one I ask."

When I stand elbow to elbow with him, he

glances my way. "We are at eighty-five percent capacity already."

I nod and pat him on the shoulder. "Let me know if you need reinforcements."

He laughs and nods. "I saw 'em walk in. That's a badass crew."

"Damn straight."

Weaving my way through the crowd of people already on the dance floor, I head toward the patio area. As I approach the bar, Derrick, the bartender, spots me. I hold up five fingers and point to the balcony. He gives me a head nod as he slides a drink order to a thirsty customer. I glance around the room and spot Jack in a booth with the twins. They all look pleased with the arrangement.

About half the tables are full when I step out onto the deck. The guys are sitting in the back corner. Wynona is their waitress, and she is laughing her ass off. No doubt, Mike is entertaining her with some wild story.

I walk over to the table and lean against the handrail, waiting for her to set the plate of wings down and take their orders. Everyone orders the steak. She laughs, "Meat eaters, no vegetarians here."

I look down into the parking lot and spot a candy apple red Corvette pulling in next to my Bronco. When the driver gets out, I recognize his gait and shout down. "B.A!"

He looks up and waves, "Yo, Rocket!"

"I'll be waiting for your update."

"Looking forward to it. It was a good mission." He continues into the rear entrance of the Hotel.

I turn back to the table as Wynona backs out. She asks, "Do you want steak too?"

"Affirmative. Rare."

"Do you know what Nina will have?"

"Yes, but I'll let her order for herself."

Wynona says, "I'll bring Nina's wine when she arrives, then take her order."

"Thank you."

"Yep."

I take the empty seat, and Jocko slides an open beer to me. Mike laughs and says, "You're learning."

I give him a head nod as I reach for the chicken wings and pile a hand full on my plate.

Jocko asks, "Was that Brody Andrews?"

"Affirmative."

"Have you asked him to join us?"

"He has a date."

"I meant the team."

"Not yet."

"But you intend to?"

"Affirmative."

"Good. He would be a good fit."

"So," Dirk asks, "I take it the three of you all served on Alpha together?"

Mike answers, "Affirmative. Nina as well."

"And the dog?"

"What dog?" Jocko asks.

Dirk laughs and nods at Lucifer lying under the table. "That one."

"He's a retired, decorated, combat war hero, buddy. He ain't a dog."

Dirk smirks, "Well, I stand corrected and answered."

Everyone laughs.

Jocko nods and says, "Just wait until you see him work. Then you'll know, he's not a dog. He's an MPC."

Dirk laughs, "I was just poking you, Jocko. I read up on each of you before I joined up, including the retired, decorated, combat war hero sleeping under the table. Honestly, I'm excited to get to work with y'all."

Jocko gives him a knuckle bump. "I was poking you too. Hardcore told us not to cut you any slack just because you're a flyboy."

Dirk smirks, "Just wait until you see my work, then you'll know I'm not just another flyboy."

Mike laughs out loud. "Touché!"

The next ten minutes, Dirk entertains us with antics from his days serving with Hardcore, and when Wynona brings our food, Mike entertains us with his version of events for Dirk's benefit while we eat.

When Nina walks onto the deck, I don't hear another word being said. All I can hear is the sound of my heart rate increasing and drowning everything else out. She looks absolutely gorgeous. Her hair is piled on top of her head in a bun, and she's dressed in an off the shoulder, open back, red silk dress with red stiletto heels. My cock hardens immediately as the urge to meet her halfway, turn her around, march her back to my suite to give her a good hard fucking weighs heavy on my mind.

Mike's whistle and his, "Damn, woman! You clean up good," breaks through my trance.

She cocks that eyebrow at him, and he throws up his hands, making everyone laugh.

She walks over to me, and I reach for her. My hand settles on her bare thigh as she places her hand on my shoulder. "Bri just called. She's asked me to come over. Bethany's suffering a little PTSD."

"Of course." I stand, "I'll walk you out."

"I'm sorry to bug out, but I'm sure you all understand."

Jocko nods to her, "Of course, she was traumatized."

Mike says, "Well, if you're not going to be here to dance with, I'm going to go FaceTime with my family, then crash and burn on the bed."

Dirk agrees. "Sounds like the smart plan of action."

Nina slips her hand in mine, and we all walk out together.

Fourteen

Crockett

I hear a "hooyah" just as I walk back inside and see Brody standing outside the dinner theater on his phone. I throw up my hand and wave. "Did I hear a hooyah?"

He grins. "Yes, sir! You sure did." He walks to me with his hand outstretched.

I clasp it firmly and pump it. "Good to see you, Brody."

"You too."

"So, you've gotten good news?"

"Yes, my application for OCS [Officer Candidate School] has been accepted."

"That's awesome news! Congratulations! When do you leave?"

"I don't know the details yet, just that I'm in."

"Well, this calls for a celebration! Come on," I throw my arm around his shoulders. "Let's go to the bar and toast this amazing news."

He glances back at the dinner show but doesn't say anything about the girl, Lizzy, so I assume she didn't pan out.

When we step in the elevator, I immediately begin his job interview, just shooting the shit with him. "So, where are you stationed?"

"Virginia Beach."

When we step off, I introduce Brody to Damien as Badass and inform him, he earned that name in bars, not as a SEAL on the battlefield.

The smirk on Damien's face makes us both laugh, so I give my bouncer a little of our history. "I met Brody in a bar fight and told him if he was such a badass, he should go prove it by becoming a Navy SEAL."

"Let me guess," Damien says, "You two were the ones fighting."

Brody smiles, "Affirmative."

"Well, who won?"

We answer at the same time, "Hooyah."

Damien laughs and shakes his hand. "I got your back, but let's not live up to that reputation tonight."

Brody laughs, "As long as I'm not provoked, everyone will leave with their teeth intact."

As we make our way to the VIP area, several people shout my name, and I throw my hand up in acknowledgment. When we arrive at my booth, Amanda is already waiting on us. She asks Brody, "What will you have, cutie?"

His eyebrows shoot up, and he laughs. "Bud in a bottle."

"You sure you don't want a frosted mug?"

He laughs again, "Nope. If a fight breaks out, I'll have a weapon."

She looks him up and down appreciatively, and I think Brody just might get lucky tonight anyway. She teases him, "I should have known you were a SEAL. Coming right up." Then she spins around and walks off.

He leans over to me and grins, "Before I start

entertaining you with war stories, what have you been up to?"

"Nothing good, but that's about to change."

"Let's hear it."

Amanda returns with a bucket of beer, and I pull two from the ice but have to wait before I slide one to Brody. His eyes are focused on something or someone else. I follow his line of sight, but nothing is obvious.

When he looks back, I slide the bottle to him. We twist the tops off, and I raise mine in salute. "First, a toast to your acceptance into the elite of the elite. Hooyah!"

"Hooyah!"

We drain our beers, racing to finish first, and slam the empty bottle down onto the table at the same time.

I laugh. "Either I'm getting slower, or you're getting better." I slide round two to him as I start my sales pitch. "I wanted to speak to you about a special project I've been working on. It seems there is a need right here at home for our skills."

"Really?" He leans in, listening, but his eyes are searching the dance floor for someone. It is probably Lizzy, the girl he wanted the room by.

SEALs are not quitters, and if he wants her, he won't stop until he has her.

I decide not to tell him about Bethany's rescue. He isn't married and doesn't have children, so the emotional impact will not be as potent as sharing the business vision with him and giving him a viable option.

"A few months ago, I was approached by a family whose son and his girlfriend had been taken hostage while on a mission trip. Long story short, they hired me to put together an extraction team. We went in, did a snatch and grab, and brought them both home safely. Word has spread, and I've had multiple missions requested, so I'm putting together a team of special operators."

He rocks back in his seat. "And you were going to ask me to join you?"

"Affirmative." I open two more beers and push him one of them. "But if you're going to become an officer, you'll have to tack on more years and another tour." I leave the implication hanging that he will be missing out on something great.

He mulls over what I've said, then tips the

beer up, drains it, and says, "It will, but I like options. Tell me more."

"Brody, I'd love to have you join my team. I would compensate you well for your time. When you're on a mission, you will get a cut of the contract. When you're not on a mission, you will be required to train regularly, of course, and you'll have a set salary that we can discuss later. Other than that, you'll have all the free time you want."

He lifts his beer and takes a long draw. "Who's the money man backing you?"

"His name is Aurelius Moore. He's a venture capitalist, former Army Aviator, Apache pilot. We go way back."

"Do you have training facilities?"

"Yes, Aurei bought a ranch outside of Vegas."

"Vegas, huh?" He grins.

"Yeah. It is definitely a perk." I grin with him.

"Who else have you recruited?"

"Mike Franks, Jack Black, Jocko Malone and Lucifer, and Nina Fox. They all served with me on Alpha."

"Sounds like an impressive group."

"They are. Does it sound like something

you'd be interested in?" I take a long draw from my beer.

"You definitely have given me something to think about. I love what I do, but I'll give it consideration."

"Fair enough," I tell him and sit back in my seat. After I watch him searching the dancers again, I ask, "So tell me about your last mission?"

He opens his mouth to say something but doesn't. Instead, he presses it into a hard line. His brows darken. I know that look. That is his badass bar brawler face. He shifts in his seat and reaches for another beer.

I look again to see what has him irked, and I spot her—a very curvy, gorgeous girl dancing with another man. I laugh, knowing Badass won't let that stand, and I poke the bear into taking action. "I'm betting from the look on your face that *Miss* Lizzy Mayer is out there dancing with another man."

"Yes" is the only word he says before draining the beer. Then he slams that dead soldier on the table and begins recounting his last mission to me without taking his eyes off her. He is just getting to the good stuff when he stiffens, and I look back out to see Lizzy pinned between two men. She is looking for an escape, and they are rubbing their junk all over her under the pretense of dancing. If it were happening to anyone other than the girl Badass has a thing for, I would signal Damien to come to her rescue and throw their asses out, but I know B. A. will serve them up and make them pay in a way Damien isn't allowed to.

His jaw sets, and he says through clenched teeth. "Later, Jeff."

I offer, knowing he won't want help and certainly won't need it. "Let me know if you need my help. I'll send my boys over there."

"I got this." He tells me and storms into the crowd.

I laugh, knowing he sure as hell does.

I signal to Amanda to close my tab out. While I wait for her, I send a text to Nina.

HOW ARE THEY DOING?

THEY WILL BE ALL RIGHT.
IT WILL JUST TAKE TIME.

ETA [ESTIMATED TIME OF ARRIVAL]?

I'm going to hang around for at least another hour. Just to be sure Bethany is sound asleep.

Wake me when you come to bed.

Copy that.

Out.

<3

Fifteen

June 2, 2010
Just after midnight

———

Crockett

———

My phone rings, and I jerk awake. As I sit up and grab it, I reach for Nina. She isn't in bed.

A call coming in at night? My girl not by my side?

Not good.

I stifle the emotion that threatens and focus on the number calling. It is Hardcore.

"Crockett," I answer.

"Crockett, Hardcore. I've got a situation in Alabama."

I throw off the covers at the urgent tone in his voice.

"What kind of situation?" I ask, standing.

"My sister-in-law is missing."

"Give me the details." I walk to the closet and grab my rucksack as he explains that there was an apparent break-in at his sister's home. She was attacked and knocked in the head. Before she lost consciousness, she called him.

I throw my gear on the bed.

When he arrived, he found her alive, but her wife was not there. A K9 tracked her scent and, based on the direction of travel from the house and the fact that her phone was found on the street, they concluded she did not choose to go willingly.

"Roger that. The team is here at the Hotel. We had a week of training scheduled. We will leave San Diego within the hour." I pause, but he doesn't say anything. "Don't worry, Hard. We will find her. Crockett out."

I stare at my phone and decide my immediate course of action. I call Nina.

She answers on the second ring. Her voice is sleepy. I see her bed hair, puffy eyes, and pouty mouth, and my heart hardens. I tell myself, 'Stay frosty!' I have to stay focused on the mission and lock down my emotions.

She apologizes. "Rocket, I'm sorry. I fell asleep on the couch with Bri. I'll be right there."

"Foxtrot, listen up." I tell her, "Hardcore just called. There is a possible kidnapping in Alabama. Get here now."

"What? Oh my God!" I can see her eyes sharpen and her whole demeanor changes, and I can hear it in her voice. The targeting officer is back. "I'm on my way."

She hangs up, and I dial Mike. "Mike, there's a situation in Alabama that needs our skills. Wheels up to The Chicken Ranch in one. Briefing in the lobby in ten."

"Copy that." He answers. "I'll notify the others."

I call Meghan. "Ambassador, we have our first mission. Unfortunately, it is with Hardcore in Alabama. ETA to the Chicken Ranch, two hours. Make sure License understands this is not a drill. We are live."

"Copy that. I will notify Dark Thirty too."

"Foxtrot and I will video chat to discuss our game plan once we are airborne."

"Copy that. I'll be on-site in fifteen."

When I exit the elevator, the team is there, waiting. Nina is still ten minutes away. They are huddled together on a wall, off the check-in counter, opposite the lobby sitting area.

I stroll over to them, "Nina is ten minutes out. Here's the situation. Hardcore's sister-in-law has vanished. Right now, he suspects she was taken but doesn't know at this point by who. We will fly to the Chicken Ranch. Gear up, board the jet, and have boots on the ground in Alabama by early morning."

The lobby doors open, and Brody and Lizzy walk in. I throw my hand up, and he heads my way. I step away from the team and walk over to them.

Mindful that Lizzy is a civilian and fresh to Brody, I smile at her so as not to frighten her with my intensity, and I address Brody as a businessman would.

"B.A., I just received a call. A friend of mine needs my services."

"These guys part of your team?" He nods in their direction.

"Yeah, we're assembling for a briefing before we fly down." I stick my hand out. "We'll catch up later."

"No worries, brother. It was good seeing you." He clasps it, then gives me a bro hug, which I take as a good sign he is considering my offer. "Good luck. Hope the mission is successful."

I nod, "It will be."

I walk back to the team. Their eyes are all on Badass. I tell them, "Go do what you have to do and be back here in twenty."

They disperse, and I wait for Nina to arrive.

When she walks in, my cock reacts.

Damn, woman! This is going to be a real fucking challenge. I can control my mind and put a steel band around my heart, but my cock is proving to have an uncontrollable wild side for her.

I smirk. Who knew one woman could hold his attention with such devotion?

She is still wearing that killer red dress. Her

hair is down and messy. The look on her face is all business, and I realize she will be the one who has ultimate control over my rocket. He will behave for her. He will do anything for her. I smirk again.

She puts her hand on my arm, leans up for a peck, which I gladly give her, then says, "Status update?"

I take her hand and lead her to the elevator. When the doors close, I pull her into my arms and kiss her. At first, she resists, but then I feel her body mold itself into mine.

With her simple show of affection, that little peck on my lips hardened my cock, and it reminded my heart that we weren't restricted anymore, and my heart forced my brain to surrender the unnecessary discipline. I don't have to control anything.

When the time for ground zero is at hand, we will be focused on the mission. But right now, we have fifteen minutes of personal time left together before the mission clock starts, and we will be separated until the job is done. No matter how long it takes.

When the elevator doors open, I pick her up, carry her inside my suite, walk straight to the bed, and drop her on it. I shuck off my pants, and my cock springs out. She reaches for me, and I collapse on top of her. Our lips lock in a fierce kiss as I push her dress up and prepare to pound her.

Damn! Commando! She isn't wearing any panties.

Pre-cum surges forward as I enter her naked zone and drive my rocket home. I pound her so hard and so fast with the need of a man who knows who he loves and understands the dangers of the mission that the bed bangs the wall, and the mattress bounces with recoil.

When I shoot my wad into her, I speak the truth against her ear, "I fucking love you, Nina Fox."

Her moan is loud and long as her orgasm arrives. Then she clings to me and holds me tight against her. "I know."

We breathe together, letting our heartbeats return to normal. When I tense against her to get up, she squeezes me tight, holding me in place, and whispers softly in my ear. "I fucking love you too, Jeff Crockett."

The surge of emotion that soars through me is mind-boggling, and I collapse back on top of her, kissing her lips, her eyes, her face.

She starts to giggle and says, "I wasn't expecting this reaction."

I chuckle too and stop. I stare for a moment into her eyes, and we both know it is time to get down to business.

Sixteen

Live Oak, Alabama
June 2, 2010

———

Crockett

———

When the jet lands, everyone is ready to roll.

Nina and Meghan are at The Coop. License To Own and Micah are aware that they are on standby till further notice.

When the hatch opens, we are standing at

the ready. I exit first. Good. The two black SUV rentals are here. I head over to the drivers and sign their papers as Mike, Jack, Jocko, and Dirk load the gear into the back. Mike, Dirk, and I take the lead vehicle with Jack, Jocko, and Lucifer in the other.

We head straight for downtown and made good time.

My phone dings.

> COME TO
> NIK'S MMA GYM
> 555 E MAIN STREET.

I read it out loud to Mike and forward it to Jack. Then cue it up on the vehicle's navigation.

Mike says, "That can't be too hard to find."

I smirk as the program responds with an estimated arrival time of three minutes.

I reply to Hardcore.

> EN ROUTE. ETA 3 MINUTES OUT.

When we pull into the parking lot, Mike drives to the storefront marked 'Nik's Mixed

Martial Arts Gym.' It is located in a small strip next to a free-standing Publix grocery store. There is a local donut shop, called 'Donut Dilemma,' on the opposite end of the gym, and a dance studio, named 'I Hope You Dance' in-between them.

When we exit the vehicles, Jack makes a smart comment about how these three things don't go together, and Jocko responds with, "You gotta love small towns, man."

I open the door to the gym and enter to find Hardcore standing next to two other men. One is in sweats, and the other is wearing a t-shirt that reads, "Donut Dilemma."

The team files in behind me and stands respectfully waiting while I take the lead.

Before the small talk and introductions, I want to know, "Anything new to report?"

Hardcore steps forward with his hand out, and I shake it as he shakes his head. "No. I am glad you made it. I am ready to get going."

I nod, then reach over to shake the closest man's hand, introducing myself. "Crockett."

"Justin Davis, Danger. Hooyah."

I grin. "Ah. Good news."

Hardcore nods as I hold my hand out to the

other man. He takes it and pumps it. "Nik Smirnov. This is my gym."

I nod as I look around. "Thanks for letting us use it. It is a good base."

Then Hardcore turns his attention on the team. Dirk steps forward and, as they embrace, says, "I'm here for you, brother. Whatever you need."

"Thanks, buddy." He turns to Nik and Justin. "Dirk Sam and I are old friends from flight school, and Siri and his wife, Piper, were college roommates."

They nod, and Dirk steps back. I introduce the others to Nik and Justin.

"Mike Franks, Mr. Mom."

Mike nods.

"Jack Black, Hammer."

"Jocko Malone, K9 handler for Lucifer."

Jocko gives a head nod and speaks directly to Hardcore. "Angel was a good student."

"Did you bring Lucifer?"

"He is waiting in the car."

Nik says, "He is welcome here too."

Jocko steps out, and we watch in silence as he opens the door and his solid black Belgian Malinois leaps out. To say that Lucifer is intense is an understatement. The dog has serious skills.

When Jocko opens the door, Lucifer walks in with him and sits at his side, staring up at him.

Hardcore laughs, "Lucifer suits him."

Jocko chuckles and looks down at his boy, "Let's just say that if he could 'hooyah,' he would."

Just then, the door opens, and a blonde woman with a big white bandage on her head walks in. She must be Hardcore's sister. There is no mistaking the likeness. She ignores all of us and speaks directly to him. The urgency in her voice overrides her rudeness. Her wife is gone. Nothing else matters.

"Bee was kidnapped. She was taken by at least two men."

Hardcore walks over to her and puts his arms around her. "I know. Don't worry. We're going to find her."

They hold each other for a moment, then she steps back and surveys who else is in the room. She doesn't say anything but nods her gratitude.

Hardcore touches her shoulder, and she looks back at him. "Ann, Siri is missing too."

"What? Oh my god! No!" Her face crumples

with her emotions, and Hardcore's reflects her anguish.

I step forward, needing to get their emotions under control. "Sit down, Ann. We do not need you to fall out. Time is crucial. Let's go back to what happened at your house."

Hardcore takes the chair Justin pushes to him, and Ann sits in it. He offers another, but Hardcore shakes his head. He stands next to her instead.

Ann takes a deep breath and starts. "Bee has been acting really weird lately."

"Drugs?" Jack asks.

She shrugs. "I don't know. Maybe." She looks out the window. "We've been fighting nonstop over stupid shit, so it is possible."

"We went to bed. Something woke me up. I don't know what. Bee was not in bed. She has started smoking again, so I thought she was probably outside on the front porch having a cigarette. I got up to look out the window to see if she was out there. I saw her on her phone. Then I saw a man dressed in black hit her on the back of the head. She fell, but he caught her and carried her into the woods. I grabbed my phone and my gun from the nightstand. Suddenly, I felt a sharp pain and dropped to my knees. When I came to, I was disoriented. I still had my phone, but my gun was gone. I called my brother, then passed out again. I woke up in the hospital." She shakes her head. "What the fuck!"

Seventeen

Crockett

I ADDRESS THE NEXT QUESTION TO Hardcore. "What happened with Siri?"

He shakes his head, and his words tell me his emotions are threatening to spill over. "We fucked up. That's what happened." He looks over at Jocko. "We left Angel at home."

Jocko nods and says, "It's okay, brother. Don't look back. Move forward."

He nods and continues. "Siri and I went to The Stallion. She was filling in for a friend. An hour in, Ann called me. I told Siri I would check on her, and I would let her know. I called and informed her that Ann was hurt. That I was going to the hospital with her. But Siri's phone was in the back of my truck. However, at this point, I did not know that. Siri called and then texted from Red's phone that she was going with the girls to Donut Dilemma."

Mike asks, "Is that their routine?"

Justin nods, "Yes. We give the dancers an early bird discount and let them come in to unwind while Farrah and I are cooking."

"How many girls last night?"

Hardcore answers. "Five plus Siri, but they didn't make it. They were run off the road, lost control, went down an embankment, and crashed."

"How do you know that?"

"Justin and I found the crash site, and the side of the SUV has damage and paint transfer consistent with another vehicle sideswiping it."

"Continue."

"The driver was killed in the crash." He looks at Ann. "Red died on impact."

She shakes her head and bites her lip—tears threatening again.

"Everyone else had vanished. The car doors

were left open. Nothing was taken. Cash, phones, and purses were left behind. It looked like a snatch and grab."

His phone rings.

I tell him, "Answer it." I don't add, 'it could be kidnappers asking for a ransom,' but I don't have to.

His eyes lock with mine. "Moore speaking."

The silence in the room is deafening. The only sound is Lucifer hassling.

He drops his head, closes his eyes, and says, "Siri! Thank God!"

Everyone takes a deep breath, then he says, "I am at Nik's gym. Where are you?"

She answers somewhere.

"Are you hurt?"

He looks at me, and I see the relief on his face as he shakes his head that she isn't. She is okay. I motion for him to put her on speaker, and he tells her as he taps the button.

"I am putting you on speaker."

We hear the sweet, southern voice of the star that sings like Whitney Houston say, "My God, what a fucked-up night, Aurei. I have to call the police. Fuck. I don't know where to start. Fuck."

She starts to cry, and he speaks softly to her. "Siri, breathe, baby. You got this."

She sobs for a moment, then she says. "I'm sorry. I just need a fucking hug from my man." I can hear the strength and fight in her voice. Then we listen to her taking deep breaths, getting her shit together.

Aurei smiles, "Good girl!"

She blows a deep breath out and says, "Okay. I'm good." But she does it twice more before she speaks again. She asks, confused. "Why am I on speaker?"

I take the lead. "Siri, Crockett speaking. Aurei has called my team in. We know your friends were taken, and we are going to find them. Can you tell us what happened? We know the vehicle was sideswiped."

She takes another deep breath. "We were hit, and Red lost control. I was knocked out, and when I came to, there were men at the car.... Red was dead... They thought I was too injured and left me behind. My face is black and blue from the airbag, but I'm okay.... I got lucky...." She takes another deep breath before she says, "They took the others."

Hardcore and I stare at each other, stunned by this news.

I tell her, "Siri, everyone thought you were taken by traffickers."

"I wasn't, but I think the other girls were. We were definitely targeted."

Hardcore asks, "What happened to you?"

She says, "Aurei. Take a deep breath. Stay calm."

His jaw clenches and his face fills with anger. "Ruth?"

"Yes, but she is dead, and so is Rachael."

Ann blurts out. "Oh, my God! What happened?"

"They must have seen us run off the road. They waited until the others left. Then they came down and found me. They took me at gunpoint back in the woods to Darren Martin's hunting cabin. They were going to make Aurei pay ransom to release me. But ...." She takes another deep breath and blows it out slowly. "But I convinced them that taking my necklace and going to Mexico without involving Aurei was a better plan."

I have to admit. I am impressed. She kept her cool during the ordeal.

Mike says softly, "What a woman," making Hardcore smile.

She continues, "Ruth decided she didn't want to take Rachael, so she shot her, and when she tried to remove my necklace.... Well, I didn't let her. I choked her."

"Good job!" Jack says.

Hardcore praises her, "You did good, baby."

"I know. I promised to protect our Us, and I kept my word. I just wish they would not have been so stupid."

He smirks and brags, "That's my girl."

I tell her, "Siri, we are going to call the police and have them come here to get your statement. You need to know that Bee was taken last night too. Probably by the same gang."

"Oh, my fucking God! Is Ann alright?"

"I am here, doll. I took a hit too, but I'm good."

I ask her, "How far out are you now?"

"Five minutes."

"Okay." I motion to the team to get things ready and look at Justin and Nik.

Siri's voice says, "Aurei?"

"Yes, Wild Thang?"

"Take me off speaker."

He smiles, holds the phone to his ear, and walks outside.

The team move to the stacked tables and take two off.

I walk over to Nik. "We need to set up our command center."

Eighteen
Coq Blockers

June 5, 2010
4 AM

Crockett

Nina's voice comes over the Manpack radio.

"One. Check-in."

I smile. That's her way of saying, "Good morning, Love."

"One here." That's my way of answering, "ditto."

"Status update?"

"Alive and well."

She laughs. "Roger that."

Mike keys his comm. "Two here. Alive and well, if you give a shit."

She laughs, "Of course, you are. A motherfucker like you just won't die. And, of course, I do. Just not in the same way."

He laughs. "Copy that."

I reply. "Two and I are onsite enjoying a nice sugar rush compliments of Donut Dilemma."

She laughs. "I take it all is quiet on the Alabama home front?"

"Affirmative. No activity."

"Thermal says they are inside, so sit tight."

"Roger wilco. We are hunkered down."

"Commando out." She says, and I crack up laughing.

Mike rolls his eyes. "I swear, I don't know which is worse. Watching the two of you pine for each other for years, or having to listen to the two of you tease each other incognito."

I laugh, "Well, I sure as hell know which one was worse!"

He chuckles. "Seriously, brother. I'm happy for you two. We all are. You two were made for each other."

I grin. "The fit is pretty special."

He rolls his eyes again.

Brody keys his comm. "So ... I know I'm six and not in the loop on the team dynamics, but did she just say, 'commando' as in ... you know, commando?"

Justin keys ups, "That's what I heard. I think the new additions need to be brought up to speed."

Mike chuckles and moves his hand to key his comm again, but Jack beats him to it. "They're fucking."

I roll my eyes, and Mike dies laughing.

Jocko keys up, "Are there any donuts left?"

I respond. "Affirmative."

He answers, "On my way over."

We are staked out at a small farmhouse about four miles from the city limits of Live Oak. The location was pinpointed last night, and we surrounded it before midnight. Now, we play the waiting game on visual confirmation that the women are, in fact, inside.

As we watch, I think about whether this first

case will be the norm or if it will be a unique situation. As military special forces, we did not operate inside the United States but rather carried out covert missions overseas. Although the tactics are identical, and the rules of engagement are similar. Do not fire unless fired upon. We are not operating outside the law here. Something that will need to be addressed in the after-action report for future missions on US soil.

On this mission, we have a workaround. Since Live Oak is a small town without a municipal police force and relies on the sheriff's department for law enforcement.

Sheriff Deputy Zane Lockhart, a former SEAL himself, took Siri's statement at the gym, and when he met us, he realized the sheriff's office could take advantage of having our teamwork the kidnapping with him.

We were deputized and went to work, processing the crime scene. All hard evidence collected was sent to a police lab in a larger neighboring town for analysis.

Then the next day, we hit the pavement looking for perp information. Surveillance cameras are not on every corner, so gathering intel was slow. But most everyone knows each other, and they were willing to speak to us, so we were able to ascertain some critical details on the traffickers.

But the real breakthrough came through when B. A. joined us.

"I am in."

"That is fucking fantastic news! How soon can you start?"

"I am on thirty days leave right now. I'm going to call my commander as soon as we hang up and start the paperwork. I should be out before my leave is over."

"Man, timing is everything. I am going to need your expertise immediately."

"What do you need me to do?"

"I need you in Alabama to work up a profile for me."

"That is what I do, and I am damn good at it too."

"I'm counting on that. I don't have all the facts yet, but it looks like a snatch and grab by human traffickers. Meghan Meadows or Nina Fox will contact you with flight information."

Hardcore hired a jet to fly him straight here. On the flight, he was brought up to speed, and the first contribution he made was pivotal.

He recommended putting Siri under hypnoses to see if she could give a physical description of the men she saw. She agreed, and I sat in on the session. It was remarkable what she remembered.

Meghan took her description, made a composite of the two men, then ran it through facial recognition software. Once they were identified, she scanned the social media platforms and found them. They were actively recruiting young women between the age of twenty-one and thirty-five for overseas modeling gigs.

"See the world and earn a living.
You pay for nothing, we cover your cost,
and take a percentage of your fee."

"Unhappy with your circumstances?
Wish you could get away?
Too much stress in your life?
Take a European vacation on us."

Nina informed us, "We will have no problem finding our next mission. There are thousands of comments and tens of thousands of likes."

Once Brody arrived, he reinterviewed Ann, and she gave him her wife's email password. Then Dark Thirty was able to recover some deleted correspondence with Bee, Ann's wife, and Rita, one of The Stallion dancers. They had signed up for the modeling gig, but then they changed their minds at the last minute.

The emails from the 'modeling agency' addressing her 'no show' became darker and darker. Warning her that their gigs had been booked, and she had signed a binding contract. "You cannot back out."

The pieces of the puzzle fell into place after that, and we determined that the women were being held in the farmhouse we have surrounded.

Nineteen

5:15 AM

Crockett

"Check-in," I instruct my team, and they sound off in order.

Mike keys up, "Two, ready."
Jack says, "Three, ready."
Jocko, "Four, ready."
Justin, "Five, ready."

Brody, "Six ready."

Zane, "Seven ready."

From my vantage point up a tree on the perimeter, I look through my sniper scope and scan the windows with its night vision. The green glow shows there is no movement.

Nina's familiar, steady voice says in my ear, "Thermal indicates two are in the living room, and eight are in the master bedroom."

"Good copy," I respond. "Ten total inside."

"Affirmative." She confirms.

She adds, "Be advised, there is a vehicle approaching."

"Activate body cams, boys."

Nina tells me. "Confirmation of seven body cams activated.

A few seconds later, headlights illuminate the drive below, then go off.

She tells us, "Thermal indicates there are three passengers."

When the car comes to a stop, the occupants sit in the dark and wait.

Mike says, "I have visual on the three. Two men. One woman. The vehicle is a luxury sedan."

A few seconds later, Nina shares, "Heads up. There is movement inside the house."

I scan the windows again but see nothing.

She adds, "Two perps are moving freely. The other eight remain horizontal and stationary.

I reply, "Good copy. Five bad guys, eight hostages."

Nina adds, "Be advised. Another vehicle is approaching."

The headlights stay on, and when the vehicle pulls up next to the first one, Mike keys the comm.

"Vehicle one is a black luxury sedan."

When both vehicles' doors open for the occupants to exit, the interior lights illuminate the second vehicle.

Mike says, "Vehicle two is a blue refrigeration truck with a picture of a red crawfish on the side with the words "Fresh from the Louisiana Bayou" painted in large white letters . There are two additional perps."

I give the count. "Copy that. We now have seven bad guys and eight hostages."

Nina tells us. "Overwatch has pictures of the vehicles. Scanning now for registration information."

The lights around the perimeter of the house come on, and the perps casually head to the back door. I turn the night vision off on my scope and identify them with the low light, but I can't.

I announce, "No visual confirmation."

When the perps knock, the interior lights come on. The back door opens, someone steps into the doorway, speaks to them, then backs back inside, and the group follows them in.

Jack keys up his comm. "Three here. I have visual confirmation on Pimp Number One."

"Good copy, three."

The exterior lights go off. I turn my night vision back on. "Prepare to move to the secondary target location."

Nina updates, "Six pimps are standing in the living room. One pimp going to the bedroom...." She pauses then adds, "Violent confrontation."

I instruct the team. "Move forward."

From my vantage point, through my sniper scope, I watch my team in stealth mode creep across the yard and take their breach positions.

Nina continues her play by play updates. "Seven pimps and one hostage in LR [living room]. Seven remain stationary."

Zane, with his K9 Batman, Brody, and Justin,

takes their position at the front of the house. Mike, Jack, and Jocko with Lucifer post at the back.

Nina, "They appear to be arguing."

"Three, do your thing. Copy?"

"Good copy." His voice is low. He steps up to the back door, squats down, and sets his charge. Then he backs away and shields himself from the blast. He counts down for us. "Three, two, one."

Boom! The door falls off its hinges and into the house.

Batman begins barking.

Zane shouts, "Sheriffs department. Drop your weapons."

Mike, Jack, Jocko, and Lucifer surge inside.

Nina relays, "Two and Three to LR. Four to master. Shots fired. Three perps down. Dead. Four perps fleeing. Front door. One perp and one hostage kneeling in LR."

I turn my scope on the front of the house.

Zane controls a lunging Batman.

Justin stands ready at the door.

The first man charges out, and Zane releases Batman. The K9 leaps and takes him down. The man's scream is blood curdling.

Justin grabs the second man out and throws

him to the ground, dropping two-hundred-thirty pounds of SEAL onto the perp's back as he aims his weapon at his head.

Nina updates, "Four's in LR. Lucifer released."

Brody faces off with man number three. The butt of his weapon pressing into the man's forehead. The perps arms fly up in surrender.

The fourth man falls out of the door with Lucifer attached. His blood-curdling screams join the first man's.

Mike announces, "Target secure."

Nina responds, "Roger that."

I answer, "Copy that."

As I climb down from my perch, the sun is just breaking the horizon. Dirk and Hardcore pull up. They were stationed outside the perimeter and had comms, so they heard the entire takedown. I wait for them, and we enter the house without speaking.

Lucifer and Batman are stationed at each of the doorways. I speak to Luce when we walk by, "Good job, buddy! You still got it."

I glance into the bedroom to see Zane, Justin, Mike, and Jocko with the seven victims. Dirk and

I pass by, but Hardcore sticks his head inside. He asks, "Is Bee in here?"

Justin answers, "She's in the other room."

Several women say, "Thank you!"

In the living room, we find the live perps in handcuffs, kneeling on the floor with their dead accomplices blocking their escape. Jack and Brody guard them, and Dirk and I walk over to where they stand.

They aren't watching the men. They are watching the woman sitting in a straight back kitchen chair, squalling her eyes out, rocking back and forth, mumbling incoherently.

I nod toward her, "Bee?"

Brody nods and says, "She's unstable. Strung out on something. Probably meth. Could be hallucinating."

Jack says, "Her cheese has slid off her cracker for sure."

Just then, Hardcore enters the room, and the next few seconds play out in slow motion.

He stops and stares at her, wailing. Frowning, he calls her name, "Bee?"

She stops crying and looks at him. Shock and shame play across her face and everyone realizes at the same time that she isn't a victim. She was in on it.

Hardcore takes a step toward her, and his voice is deadly cold. "You had everything, and you choose this? Fuck you!"

Bee pulls a small revolver out from under her shirt and points it at him. Her hand is shaking badly.

Two red dots appear on her forehead. Brody and Jack have their weapons locked on her.

Dirk and I lunge for Hardcore at the same time.

But we are too late.

He charges forward.

A single gunshot breaks the silence.

Bee's body hits the floor.

Nina's voice asks in my earpiece, "Rocket?"

I respond. "Shot fired. Standby."

Jack and Brody lower their weapons, and I look at them to see which one just shot our CFO's sister-in-law. Their intense expressions are uncompromising.

Hardcore stops and stares down at Bee's lifeless body. There is no sympathy on his face, and I realize why his nickname is Hardcore. He hooks her with his foot and rolls her over.

Blood colors the hole in her shirt in a circle over her heart.

I key the radio. "Status update. Three dead. Four in custody. Seven hostages safe... One suicide."

"Copy that."

Epilogue

The Chicken Ranch
June 20, 2010

Crockett

Nina and I are racing our horses when I get a call from Zane. I pull mine up, and she continues, unaware I'm not in hot pursuit.

I answer, "Crockett, here."

"Crockett, Zane. I called to give you an update. You got a minute?"

"I have all the time in the world."

He details for me how the investigation into the human trafficking ring went. As it turned out, the woman perp was herself trafficked when she was a teenager, and once she was free, she sang like a canary, telling Zane everything she knew.

"By the time we finished with the arrests, it ranked as the biggest human trafficking bust in the Southeast."

"Congratulations!" I tell him. "Does that mean you're running for sheriff?"

He laughs, "No, that's a political job, and I want no part of that. But I did get a job offer."

"You can come work for me if you're looking."

He laughs, "Well, hear me out. I've received a job with the FBI to head an off the books human trafficking task force."

I smile, knowing where he is going with this. "And?"

"And I told them I didn't need a team of operators. I just needed permission to get the job done."

I laugh, "Hell, yeah!"

He laughs too. "It pays to be a winner."

The First Freedom Fest
July 4th, 2010

Nina

"You know, it's fascinating how a single choice by one man to do the right thing, followed by a decision by a group of great guys to collaborate together to make a difference, can change the lives of so many, isn't it?" I tell Siri Moore as we watch our heroes at the BBQ grill flipping the chicken and burgers over, under the direct supervision of the other grill-masters. While Jocko, Zane, and Mike's children play together with Batman, Lucifer, and Angel over the watchful eyes of Jorja, Laura, and Toccara.

She agrees, "Yes, it is."

She smiles at me, then throws her hand up, waving at Meghan, who is walking up with

Micah, and License. She is leading them over to meet the team of operators.

"So, can you give me the skinny on what happened after the raid? Rocket didn't share anything."

She smiles, "Long version or short version?"

Meghan leaves the group and heads our way.

"Better make it the long version, but wait for Meghan so I won't have to retell it to her."

Siri laughs and hugs Meghan's neck when she arrives, "Good to see you."

"You too. Did I miss anything?"

"Siri's going to give us the skinny on what happened."

Meghan rolls her eyes, "Thank god! None of the men would share anything."

Siri nods, "I know. I wouldn't know what I do if wasn't my sister-in-law." Her gaze travels over the group, and then she blows a kiss to Hardcore, who gives her a head nod.

"Is okay?"

"She's heartbroken, but she'll be fine. At least she knows it wasn't anything she did." Siri takes a deep breath and starts. "It's complicated, so bear with me. Bee had a miscarriage. knew she was upset about it and tried to get her to go to counseling, but she refused. What didn't know was Bee had a history of drug abuse as a juvenile, and to cope, she turned back to drugs and her old dealer."

She shakes her head and takes a breath. "You need to know Bee's background. Rita, one of the dancers at The Stallion taken in the wreck, and Bee were childhood friends. When Rita started dating an older guy, Floyd, he got them hooked on drugs. Bee's parents shipped her off to rehab, while Rita became a victim of trafficking. Floyd became her pimp. So, when Bee lost the baby, she called Rita to cry on her shoulder, and Rita called Floyd to help her friend cope."

"Now, that night, Bee called Rita desperate for a hit. She was scared shitless about what was about to go down."

"So, she knew?"

"Yes, she knew. was getting suspicious, and she didn't have the money for the drugs without Ann. So she agreed to be the mule and transport the girls a few days later to Mobile, Alabama, where they would be loaded onto a tanker and shipped to Mexico."

"Wow," Meghan says.

"But when Floyd got to Bee's house, he saw

Ann in the window, so he sent one of his guys inside to take Ann out. Bee went nuts, so he drugged her and took her with them."

"She was passed out in the vehicle, gagged and tied up, when the dancers were loaded after the wreck. At the farmhouse, she was put in the room with the others to sleep off her high. When she came to, she started raising hell about being tied up, so they brought her into the living room."

Siri's expression is so sad I put my arm around her. She blinks back tears and says, "Aurei said when she saw him, she knew she had fucked up her life, so she just shot herself."

Meghan asks, "What happened to Rita?"

"Well, Floyd was one of the men killed, and she looked at it at first as if she had lost everything too because she had no other loyalties to the traffickers. But Zane convinced her that she had a choice. She could choose a new life and a new identity, or she could choose to rot in jail."

I smile. "She went into witness protection?"

Siri nods, "On the condition, she completes rehab and remains clean, straight, and sober."

I give her another squeeze. "Rocket is always saying, 'Make good choices. Make better decisions.'"

She smiles, "Ain't that the truth!"

"DING, DING, DING!"

Rocket hits the small steel triangle hanging next to the grill with a small rod. When he has everyone's attention, he says, "I have a couple of announcements to make."

Everyone stops talking and gives him their attention. "First, the grub is done. But before we celebrate our freedom as Americans, I want to thank you for being here and being a part of our family. And the second announcement is that Coq Blockers has officially become a covert FBI task force. Our operational name is 'Born To Fight' and we will be operating under our very own, very special FBI agent, Zane Lockhart."

Everyone claps, and Zane raises his beer. "Hooyah!"

The response is immediate. "HOOYAH!

Rocket adds, "Now, enjoy today because tomorrow we will say, 'The Only Easy Day Was Yesterday.'"

"HOOYAH!"

Thank you for reading TARGET NINA.

I hope you loved meeting Nina and Crockett and will choose to leave a review for others.
Direct link to Amazon Review:
https://readerlinks.com/l/3626662

They make an appearance in each book in the *A FEW GOOD MEN* series.

Continue reading Jack Black's story in

TARGET LOGAN
https://readerlinks.com/l/3626710

In 2001, Logan Tisdale, a NYC socialite, was on college summer break in Galveston, TX, when she fell in love and married Jack Black, a bar bouncer.

Then tragedy struck personally and nationally.

Although their love was real, their marriage didn't survive the heartbreak.

Years later, she's a successful up-and-coming lawyer with a newspaper headline that reads:

NYC Prosecutor Logan Black deals a death blow to the Diablo Gang.

Past and present collide when the gang retaliates by kidnapping her.

Can Logan survive her captivity long enough for Jack and the Coq Blockers team to rescue her?

Prologue

Galveston, TX
SEPTEMBER 17, 2001

"Jack, I can't do this. I'm sorry. I just can't." I sob into my hands, knowing I'm breaking his heart.

He pulls me into his embrace and wraps his strong arms around me. " Shhh, Logan. Don't cry. Don't cry over me. I'm not worth it."

"Don't say that, Jack! You are worth it. It's me. I'm the one fucked up." I sob harder. "I'm so sorry! A wife is supposed to support her husband, but...." My tears overwhelm my words.

"Logan, don't blame yourself. We should never have married."

I look up at him and see his truth-stained tears.

He tries to reassure me with a smile, but his

lips quiver and my heart shatters into a thousand pieces. His thumb strokes my cheek. "Hey, just because we choose to live separate lives doesn't mean our hearts are any less bound together by love. I will always love you, Logan. If you ever need me for anything, I'll be there for you. You have my word."

"I love you too, Jack," I whisper and cling to him, knowing when he walks away, he will never come home to me again.

He lowers his lips to mine, and the thrill that this badass motherfucker always gives me stirs my soul for the last time.

He whispers against my forehead. "I'll text you my address once I know where I'll be stationed so you can send the divorce papers. I'll sign them as soon as I can and return them."

I nod, and he stares into my eyes. "I expect you to become the fiercest prosecutor New York City has ever feared. You got the goods, babe. You can do it."

Continue reading...
TARGET LOGAN
https://readerlinks.com/l/3626710

Coq Blockers Security Team

Jeff Crockett, aka Rocket
Target Nina
Chief Executive Officer (CEO)
Mission Team Leader
Former Navy SEAL Tier One
Special Warfare Operator
Alpha 1
Height: 6'5"
Weight: 260

Maximus Aurelius Moore, aka Hardcore
<u>Mr. Sexy in 9G</u>
Chief Financial Officer (CFO)

Billionaire Investor
Former Army Aviator
Apache and Blackhawk Pilot
Height: 6'0"
Weight: 200 lbs

Nina Fox, aka Foxtrot
Target Nina
Chief Operating Officer (COO)
Mission Team Commander
Former Tier One Targeting Officer
For Alpha Team

Meghan Meadows, aka Ambassador
Chief Liaison Officer (CLO)
Mission Coordination Team Member
Former Army ISA Officer

Mike Franks, aka Mr. Mom
Mission Team Member
Former Navy SEAL Tier One
Special Warfare Operator
Alpha 2
Height: 6'0"
Weight: 200 lbs

Jack Black, aka Hammer
Target Logan
Mission Team Member
Former Navy SEAL Tier One
Special Warfare Operator
Alpha 3
Height: 6'1"
Weight: 230

Jocko Malone, aka Fastball
Coming Home For Her
Mission Team Member
Special Warfare Operator
Former Navy SEAL Tier One
Special Warfare Operator
Alpha K9 handler
Height: 6'4"
Weight: 250

Lucifer, aka Luce
Coming Home For Her
Mission Team Member
Special Warfare Operator
Former Navy SEAL
Belgian Malinois

Multipurpose K9

Brody Andrews, aka Badass
Target Lizzy
Mission Team Member
Special Warfare Operator
Former Navy SEAL Tier Two
Special Warfare Operator
Height: 6'3"
Weight: 265 lbs

Justin Davis, aka Danger
Moving Back For Her
Mission Team Member
Former Marine
Height: 6'3"
Weight: 230

Zane Lockhart, aka Insane
Making Good For Her
Mission Team Member
Special Warfare Operator
Former Navy SEAL Tier Two
Special Warfare Operator
Deputy Sheriff - K9 handler

Height: 6'1"
Weight: 210

Batman, aka Bruce Wayne
Making Good For Her
Mission Team Member
Law Enforcement
Belgian Malinois
Multipurpose K9

Dirk Sam, aka Sam-I-Am
Manning Up For Her
Mission Air Support Team Member
Former Army Aviator
Apache and Blackhawk Pilot
Height: 6'2"
Weight: 225

Micah Young, aka Dark Thirty
Mission Technical Support Team Member
CIA Agent - Hacker

License To Own
Mission Team Overwatch
Drone Operator

Civilian Video Gamer

Nikolai Smirnov, aka Grappler
Opening Up For Her
Mission Team Hand-to-Hand Combat Trainer
Former MMA Champion Fighter
Height: 5'10"
Weight: 185

Jessika writing as Stingray23
HOT Military Romantic Suspense

A Few Good Men

Target Lizzy

Target Nina

Target Logan

Target Marie

Target Bella

Jessika writing as Cindee Bartholomew

The Liotine Heir

American Flyboy

Italy's Most Eligible Bachelor

Worth The Risk Series

Secret Life

Stunning Secret

Shocking Secret

Dark Secret

Twisted Secret

Startling Secret

Standalone

Twisted To Get Her

Read Jessika's newest, sexiest, and most talked about bestsellers...

LIFE IN LIVE OAK

Coming Home For Her

Moving Back For Her

Manning Up For Her

Opening Up For Her

Making Good For Her

SUCH A BOSS

Big Book Boss

Big Booze Boss

BILLION HEIR

Fraudulent Fiancee

Escaping in Glass Slippers

Accidental Amnesia

THE HARDCORE NOVELS:

SPECIAL EDITIONS

Untouchable Billionaire

Unstoppable Billionaire

Unforgettable Billionaire

THE HARDCORE COLLECTION:

TRILOGY BOXSETS

Undeniable Chemistry

Unbridled Passion

Unwavering Devotion

THE HARDCORE SERIES:

ORIGINAL SIRI'S SAGA

Mr. Sexy in 9G

The Cock-Tail Party

The Perfect Man

It's Ladies Night

The Battle is On

The Sex Pot

In Heaven at Last

A Shakeup Occurs

He's Hard Core

The End of Her

A Shakedown Happens

Family First Always

Learn more at

JessikaKlide.com

Stingray23

Top 4 Amazon Chart author of HOT romcoms Jessika Klide's alter ego, Stingray23 pens HOT Military Romantic Suspense Thrillers.

#4 Amazon Chart Author of HOT billionaire romance brings her readers the perfect blend of heat, humor, and heart.

JOIN JESSIKA'S VIP READER'S LIST
for exclusive giveaways, new release information, sales, and more.
https://jessikaklide.com/

Newsletters not your thing?
No worries.
— CONNECT ON SOCIAL MEDIA —

- goodreads.com
- facebook.com/JessikaKlideRomance
- instagram.com/jessikaklideauthor
- bookbub.com/authors/jessika-klide
- x.com/JessikaKlide
- tiktok.com/@authorjessikaklide

Stingray23.com

JessikaKlide.com

Made in the USA
Columbia, SC
21 July 2024